FIREWORKS

RGM DONALDSON

SELF-PUBLISHED BY RGM DONALDSON

ACT 1

Our Hero Meets a Stranger

CHAPTER 1

*M*agic happens. I know it does. I've felt it and experienced it. People pass off magic as luck or coincidence or being in the right place at the right time for some random reason. Magic isn't random. Hindsight being 20/20, I can see the times I was groomed for magic when I was younger. At age six, I read a book in my school library about a dog named Muffy, and it became my favorite book. I read it two or three dozen times, at least. I constantly talked about the book with my parents, dropping hints about how wonderful it would be to have a dog in the family. I named one of my stuffed animals Muffy. The stuffed animal was a bunny, but it didn't matter. I built a doghouse out of a cardboard box and construction paper, complete with a name plate over the door. Each letter of Muffy's name was scrawled in a different color crayon to show that this little house held the gold at the end of the rainbow.

My clever parents asked me all sorts of questions: what does Muffy eat and how often? When do I walk Muffy and play with her? Where does she sleep? They helped me figure out the lessons. They helped me learn what was needed without giving away for a moment what was coming. It was months later that my heart got what it wanted. Christmas morning, I woke to a huge box in the living room wrapped in red paper with a bright gold bow on the front. I didn't see that the top of the box was missing until a small black dachshund head popped up over the edge. Muffy jumped again, as high as she could, to see me, her new person. Before she could attempt a third try, I was in the box with her.

It's harder to believe in magic the older I get. Finding my husband and having my kids were beautiful spikes of magic. Those spikes are a few years back now. I feel like I'm off magic's path. I get up and do all that I'm supposed to do every day. I take care of the husband and the kids and the career. It's a wonderful life. This is the happily-ever-after part of my story.

There is a small, secret magic in my life that I feel when I make clothes for my kids. Last week, I sketched out on a lunch napkin a new fold for expandable pant legs that made me believe in unicorns again. My boys have longer legs almost daily, yet their waist sizes stay the same. I'll have to set up my sewing machine to figure out the stitching. I can see how I'll have to hold the fabric to sew the seam straight.

Stop daydreaming and watch the road, says the Administrator voice in my brain. I snap out of my magic haze to make a safe turn through a busy intersection. My inner Admin saves the day again. *You won't have time to touch the sewing machine until this weekend, so put the thought out of your head and concentrate on your driving.*

I owe so much to my Admin. Without her, my life would be chaos. She keeps me focused and on task. I met the Admin in an art class in elementary school. The art teacher, Ms. Murray, was young and pretty and she did not see a shred of merit in any of my attempts at art, ever. In fact, she'd hold my work up to the class as an example of what not to do.

Ms. Murray was strict. One day, she taught us about perspective by making us draw lines with a ruler and pencil to the exact measurements she called out while she pointed to a drawing from an art book that we were meant to copy. The lines became a road that led to a house in the distance. She showed us how we'd achieved a perspective drawing in the end, but perspective wasn't the real object of the lesson. The object was to draw the lines to her exact specified lengths. She measured all the lines on all our drawings and graded us on how close we came. The Admin sat next to me at my table for the first time that day. She kept my hands and nerves steady as I drew line after line. In the end, my drawing wasn't the best, but it wasn't the worst. Ms. Murray picked on someone else. It seems ironic that, as an adult, the Admin reminds me more and more of my young, pretty, and mean childhood art teacher.

It's true that the Admin sees me through life's tough trials, and it's true that she doesn't believe in anything unless it produces tangible results. Designing clothes and sewing, for example, has never made me any money, so she sees it as a waste of time. The Admin may not believe in magic, but how much she's helped me accomplish is a magic all its own. My husband and I are still together after fourteen years, my kids are healthy and happy, and I have a solid career. I started out as a department administrator in the tech industry when I was twenty-four. I was sat down in front of a UNIX machine and a Windows box and told to learn. My primary task was to format and publish the articles written by the industry analysts on our team. Now I manage the team of analysts and have had more work published than all the rest combined. Truthfully, my prolific publishing record is a result of how long I've been at this job. Others tend to move on after two to five years.

I miss magic. My daily routine hasn't changed in way too long. I don't want to figure out how many years I've been at this routine. The number will make me want to eat a whole cheesecake.

Though the chance of magic today is low, there is some light. Today, I am going to the dentist.

Only weirdos and masochists look forward to the dentist, says the Admin.

I like how it feels after my teeth are cleaned, I reply.

I can tell when you're lying, Gail.

I pause to think through what I say next. The answer is that going to the dentist gives me time away from my job, and time away from my job makes me happy. I could be walking lost and alone across the

Sahara for days, and it would feel like a vacation compared to the hamster wheel slog of life that is my career. The truth is, I have zero interest in software or hardware or technology trends. I don't care about the technology industry, at all, and yet I am very good at analyzing it. I also get paid very well for all the time I spend swimming in code that is meaningless to me. According to the Admin, these feelings are wrong.

I have a good job.

I work with terrific people.

I am paid well.

These are the blessings the Admin makes me repeat over and over while each passing moment spent as an industry analyst of technology adds another needle to the pincushion of my brain. The Admin doesn't see the pincushion as important, however. What is important to the Admin is that I'm committed to doing what I'm supposed to be doing.

I'm telling the truth. I love how it feels when my teeth are squeaky clean. I love running my tongue over my fresh, squeaky-clean teeth and hearing that I've done a good job with my flossing. I look forward to it every six months. You know this, I tell her.

I guess that's stupid enough to make sense.

The Admin means well. She makes sure I act right and think right. She lets me know when I mess up so I can do better next time. Sometimes her critiques can be harsh, but they're always fair. Like this one coming up: *I noticed in the mirror this morning that you're developing jowls. Plastic surgery is expensive, but we should look into it anyway.*

Ouch. Not that I have anything against plastic surgery. I always expected I'd get some work done when I was older. It just doesn't feel right to me that I should be older at forty-one.

Beyond playing hooky from work, entering the dentist's office holds another genuine treat. The receptionist, Marion, likes to decorate according to the season or for any upcoming holiday. The decorations are always her own creations too. She takes great pride in her work. The receptionist counter, the focal point of all her themes, is where she invariably places two dolls, Winnie and Claire, dressed and

staged in detailed tableaus. As we are near the end of July, I am grati-
fied to find the waiting room alive with midsummer glory. I stop just
inside the door and stare. Marion's counter displays a picnic scene
with a red-checked cloth on it and doll-sized plates and picnic acces-
sories. Winnie and Claire are dressed in denim, with straw hats to
shade their skin from the papier-mâché sun hung at the top of the
counter window. Cardboard clouds float inside light blue streamers
that start on either side of the sun and extend around the whole top
border of the room. In every corner and between the waiting room
chairs are picnic games for kids to pounce on and play. Small plastic
versions of croquet, miniature golf, and horseshoes are among the
summer bounty scattered around the floor – while Frisbees hang on
picture hooks high on the walls.

My mouth is agape and ready to sing high praise when my eyes
find Marion and see that she is dressed to match Winnie and Claire –
all three are in full denim jumpsuits with matching brass clasps at the
front of their belts. The straw hats even match. I gasp with delight and
surprise, which sends Marion into a spasm of joy. She claps her hands
and starts laughing at my stunned, happy reaction.

"I knew you'd love the outfits, Gail!" screams Marion in between
laughs.

"Did you do these yourself, Marion? They're great!"

"I found my own jumpsuit, and then making the doll clothes was
the easiest thing in the world. All I really had to do was match the
belts to make the outfits look identical."

"You do such creative work, Marion. Every time I walk in, you
surprise me with something new. You inspire me." It's true. I'm jealous
of her creative drive and outlet.

She doesn't have kids, so time and money are on her side, spouts
the Admin.

I can make time to be more creative, I counter. *It would do the kids good
to see more of my creative side.* The Admin agrees that inspiring the kids
is a worthwhile excuse for my worthless creative endeavors.

I take a few minutes to admire Marion's work with her before
settling into a chair to wait for my turn. I see the magazine rack and

pick up a *Vanity Fair*. A young celebrity I don't recognize is on the cover. I don't know who the young stars are these days and, frankly, I don't care. That has to mean I'm old.

The front door to the office opens and he walks in. I look up at him as he walks by me. He looks down into my face and smiles. I stop breathing. He walks to the counter where Marion is waiting with a bright smile. Her lipstick has been refreshed since we talked five minutes ago, and I notice now that her hair is done with near-perfect polish today.

"Hi, Steve, how are you?" asks Marion with a demure smile. Steve. I like that name. Like the Six Million Dollar Man, Steve Austin, this Steve looks faster, stronger, better.

"I'm well, Marion, how are you?" he replies as he does a 360-degree turn to look around the room at the decorations. He seems to notice everything except me. I want to clear my throat or say something witty to get him to look my way again. "Marion, this is your best work yet. I love it all." Steve said the word *love* to Marion. I see her breath catch a bit and find I'm jealous of her again. "The matching outfits are the best part," he says as he completes his revolution and brings his eyes back to Marion. She giggles out a "thank you, Steve," which ends in a happy, satisfied sigh. I feel invisible until Marion, seemingly without intending to, reminds Steve that I'm in the room.

"You may have to wait a bit today, Steve. There's another client ahead of you." Marion looks over at me and Steve follows her gaze. He sees me staring at him, but it doesn't put him off. He looks straight back into my eyes. I feel my cheeks burn, which makes me embarrassed. Without breaking his gaze, Steve says, "That's okay, Marion. I don't mind waiting." Then Steve walks over and sits down in the chair next to me. I have not been this nervous around a man since... well, since before meeting my husband, who never made me nervous. John always felt like home.

Steve looks like adventure. Tall, with broad shoulders, wearing a brown leather jacket, white shirt, and jeans. When he walked across the room, it was easy to visualize him cutting through thick jungle or wrestling a bear. Adventure is sitting in the chair next to me looking into my eyes. I want to divert my eyes but cannot. I'm mesmerized.

"Hi, I'm Steve."

"Hi," I squeak.

"And you are?"

"Very good, thank you."

He smiles. I smile in response.

"I was asking for your name."

My smile drops. My name? What is my name? I know I know it. "Gail!" Phew! I knew I had a name.

"I'm happy to meet you, Gail. Are you a fan of *Vanity Fair* or a fan of the actress on the cover?" Steve points to the magazine in my lap. Ugh. I don't want to admit that I don't know who the girl on the cover is. I'll look out-of-touch in front of Steve.

"I love *Vanity Fair*," I say. "It's one of my favorites."

"Mine too. The political articles are always worth reading. Have you been a patient of Dr. Hu's for very long?"

"Dr. Hu?"

"Our dentist," Steve reminds me. "I was just wondering if you've been a patient of hers for very long?"

I pause, searching for the answer. It's tough for my brain to both ogle Steve and maintain a conversation with him. The pause lingers too long.

"Don't worry about it," he says. "I don't have a great sense of time either."

"Dr. Hu will see you now, Gail," interrupts Marion.

It takes an effort, but I move my eyes from Steve and look over to her. She does not look happy with me. All that makeup and polish will go to waste if Steve gives his attention to me, I guess. I give a small nod that I've heard her. Well, it was nice while it lasted; time to get back to life.

"Here you go," I say as I rise from my chair and hand him the *Vanity Fair*. "You can have it. Enjoy the articles."

Steve looks down at the magazine I've handed him. I wait for a thank-you or a good-bye, but he just stares at the cover.

"Okay, well, it was nice to meet you." I take a step toward the office door but stop when I feel a hand on my arm.

"Wait," says Steve as he stands. "How'd you like to blow this off and get breakfast with me?"

My jaw drops. I hear Marion gasp and drop something. I hope it wasn't Winnie or Claire.

Over his shoulder he says to Marion, "Please put the cancellation charge for both of us on my account."

His eyes ask me if it's okay. Will I go with him? I stand there, stunned. It's so sudden. Nothing like this happens to me. Here it is. My day could be different.

Steve walks to the street door and opens it. He waits in the door-frame with his hand outstretched. "What do you say?" he asks. "A quick bite, then you can get back to your day. It'll be fun."

I find myself walking toward him. I'm not sure how, but my feet are moving. I walk past his smiling eyes and through the door.

The Admin meets me on the other side. Her stare of reproach stops me cold. I open my mouth to plead for permission to do this. I have my points ready: it's no more time than I would have spent in the dentist's chair, he'll likely pay so I won't be spending extra money, I like how I feel with him. But her stare is enough to machete through my excuses. Steve is at my side, waiting for me to start moving again. I don't want to tell him that I can't have breakfast with him. He bends down to meet my eyes.

"You have a busy day ahead, I'm sure, but I'm going to guess you didn't eat this morning?"

I shake my head no. If I speak, I'm afraid the Admin's voice will come out.

"I know a delicious crepe place down the street. Let's get some food in you."

I keep my eyes on Steve and walk past the Admin. She's infuriated that I'm ignoring her. My schedule today clearly states: dentist, work, feel guilty about not exercising, then dinner, laundry, dishes, and clean the guest room before I get into bed.

I'll get to it, I whisper to the Admin. *I'll get to it all. Right now I'm going to have breakfast with Steve and enjoy it. Afterward I'll get back to my life and have a story to smile and giggle about for weeks or maybe years. This is good for morale.*

The Admin doesn't care about my morale. *Let me remind you that you're married. If you want time out with a man, then go out with the man you married. The man you love.* She's right. What am I doing?

I look up at Steve, who looks down into my eyes, and I tell him, "I'm married."

"I figured. Your wedding ring gave that away. What's his name?"

"John."

"Is John going to mind if you have breakfast with me?"

I laugh at the thought. "No, he'll probably think it's great that I let a strange man lead me away from the dentist for crepes on Valencia Street." I let my eyes leave Steve for a moment as I remind myself that I'm on one of my favorite streets in San Francisco. The shops and eateries on Valencia are as eclectic and inviting as the city itself. I picked my dentist because she's located here. I thought getting myself to the dentist would be a good excuse to walk around and ogle at the quirky window displays, like I did pre-kids. In my twenties, I had no idea that walking and ogling could ever be a waste of time.

"I like John. Any kids?"

"Yes, two boys – Zach and Damon. They're eight and five."

"Sounds like a happy home life. What's your work?"

"I'm an industry analyst of technology software." That's all I ever say about what I do because that's all the time I want to spend talking about my job. This one line announces the salary and benefits I bring home to my family. It says I'm contributing.

I turn the tables on Steve. "What about you? Love, kids, work?"

"Not at the moment, nine-year-old girl named Aria, and I build virtual reality software scenes so multitudes of people around the world can explore new realms."

"Building new realms sounds fun," I chirp back like a giddy schoolgirl.

"It is. I once built a virtual world where a player could hit a baseball thrown by some of the greatest pitchers throughout history. That was a lot of fun. I'm not sure what I want to build next. I've got coder's block. I'm stuck for ideas. Maybe I should build this place as a virtual world. It's one of the best eateries in San Francisco, and it has Edgar."

We've stopped in front of a sweet restaurant with outdoor tables nestled inside a low, white picket fence. Painted on the large front window in gorgeous script are the words *Crepes Fairy*. Giant fairy wings are painted on the window around and behind the *Crepes Fairy* name. Steve guides me to the front door. I'm about to ask who Edgar is, when we are met right outside the door by a man I might have described as burly except for the neat style of his hair and mustache, and the pink tutu around his middle. Holding the tutu in place are simple pink satin suspenders over a pressed, white cotton shirt. He's a vision, all the way down to his white leggings and gleaming white spats over his shiny, pink dress shoes. I don't see wings, but there is no doubt that I am face-to-face with the Crepes Fairy.

"Steve!" he trumpets. Of course, the Crepes Fairy knows and loves Steve. Who wouldn't? I just met Steve ten minutes ago and…

"Edgar, you look smashing, as always," replies Steve. "I've brought a friend with me today – Gail."

"Gail, it's a pleasure to meet you." The way Edgar barely looks at me suggests otherwise. "Would you like to sit outside, Steve? The weather's perrrrfect." The way Edgar trills the word "perfect" makes me giggle. This gets Edgar's attention; he turns his whole gaze on me.

I decide to meet the Crepes Fairy where he lives and respond, "I think sitting outside would be perrrrfectly delightful." Edgar's nonplussed expression doesn't even waver. "And I would also like to say you look spectacular. Your outfit makes me hungry for a pink crepe. Do you make pink crepes?" This seems to defrost the Crepes Fairy a bit.

"As a matter of fact, I do," says Edgar. "Our Strawberry Fields crepe is pink from the strawberry juice we use in the batter. The crepe comes with our homemade whipped cream, fresh strawberries, and a raspberry-infused balsamic reduction."

"You had me at pink," I say. "That sounds brilliant. I'll have that."

The Crepes Fairy turns his attention back to Steve, and his face once again lights up like a birthday candle. "The usual, Steve?"

"Perrrfect, thanks, Edgar. We'll take a table out here."

Steve and I sit at the table nearest us. I look up into the sky and see an airplane flying across the open blue expanse.

"Dreaming of far-off places?" asks Steve.

"Yes, often," I admit. "Seeing an airplane makes me happy. When I see an airplane, I make a secret wish to be on it. I envy the people who are going somewhere."

"Where would you like to go?" asks Steve.

"I don't know. Anywhere, really."

"I can get you to Vancouver."

CHAPTER 2

"*V*ancouver?" I ask Steve.

"Yes, I can take you to Vancouver today."

"Today?" I ask him.

He's crazy. Get up and leave, orders the Admin.

"If not now, when?" Steve asks me this question, but I cannot make sense of it. Steve says he can take me to Vancouver. What does that mean?

"Today?" I ask again.

"Now. I have a pilot's license and a plane, and I can get us to Vancouver in the next ninety minutes. Have you seen Vancouver?" Steve asks.

"No," I reply. The Admin's response is louder.

NO! You have work. You have family. You have laundry to do that if you don't do your kids won't have clean underwear or clean school shirts tomorrow and then what kind of mother are you? You don't know this man! The Admin is screaming at me.

"Steve." I say his name aloud to prove to the Admin I at least know his name.

"Yes?" Steve replies.

"I can't." These words squeak from my lips. I realize I don't want to say them.

You want to say them, the Admin makes clear.

"You can, Gail. You can eat your pink crepe that is about to be delivered by a talented crepe-making man wearing a pink tutu. You can fly with me to Vancouver and see something today you've never seen before, and you can trust me to get you back before your kids are home from school."

"You make it all sound so easy," I fire back. I sound angry. Am I angry? It's been a while since I yelled at anyone other than my kids.

"It's just that easy. Come with me. If not now, when?"

"I'll tell you when." Yep, I'm angry. "After I talk to my husband first, after I ask my manager for the day off, after I inform my clients of where my projects for them stand, and, most important, after I hug my kids and tell them I love them in case you're not such a great pilot and the plane crashes."

Bravo! applauds the Admin. This rush of indignation almost lifts me from my seat and has me marching back to my car, except the Crepes Fairy appears with our plates and sets them before us with a flourish. "Here's one Strawberry Fields crepe for Gail and an Indiana Jones crepe for Steve. Is there anything more I can bring you? Coffee or tea? A mimosa?"

"No thanks, Edgar, I'm flying today," pronounces Steve.

"That sounds fun. Where are you off to?" Edgar inquires.

"A day trip to Vancouver for fun, to see the city," says Steve. "That is, if Gail will come with me."

I want to scream. I look up at Edgar, ready to give him my seat on the plane. I see in his longing eyes that a trip to Vancouver with Steve is exactly what he wants to do today. I should jump at this chance to duck out, but seeing Edgar's willingness just pisses me off. Why? Because I'm just as obvious as Edgar. I want to go to Vancouver and I want handsome Steve to fly me there. I want to blow off my day and have an adventure.

TRAITOR, spits the Admin.

"The crepes look delicious, Edgar, thank you. I think we're good for now," says Steve. Edgar heaves a sigh, then turns and goes back inside. Steve chooses not to press me. His eyes shift to the food in front of him. He picks up his fork and starts to eat. I have no idea what to do now.

"Please eat – your pink crepe looks fantastic," says Steve.

I look down at my crepe. It does, in fact, look fantastic. The balsamic reduction is laid out in lines that form a grid across a blanket of pink crepe. In each square of the grid is a slice of strawberry tucked in with whipped cream. There is no denying that this is a Strawberry Fields crepe. I look over at Steve's plate and see that his is a dark brown crepe – must be chocolate – and it's in the shape of a fedora. Thick, dark chocolate syrup lines the outer edge of the crepe and then crosses it like the band of leather on Indy's hat. The best part, though, is how the dark syrup line trails off the hat and onto the side of the plate, ending in what looks like the tail of a whip. The Crepes Fairy really knows his stuff.

In my dazed confusion over flying to Vancouver, I make a decision. I decide to eat my crepe. I pick up my fork and carefully remove a square of the grid and then eat it. It tastes as good as it looks. I melt a bit and even make a yummy sound, "mmmmm." I start cutting off another square with my fork and find myself pleased to be harvesting this field.

Steve smiles – I don't look at him but I can tell he's smiling. He says, "Sounds like you like it. I'm glad. It's a relief really. I would hate to start this day with food you don't like. Though, the Crepes Fairy has always been a sure bet for a great meal."

Don't let your defenses down, coaches the Admin. *You're not going to Vancouver. You're going to eat your crepe and go home to your work and to John. Vancouver is a ludicrous idea. Just talk about the freaking crepes with this guy and then we're leaving.* The Admin is livid. Though I am still upset as well, I would like to enjoy my clandestine breakfast. I'm not supposed to be here. I should be in a dentist's chair.

"The crepe is delicious," I tell Steve. Then I search for something to talk about, anything but planes and Vancouver. "According to Edgar, that's your usual order here, so I guess you're a frequent customer?"

"My daughter and I come here every Saturday morning," says Steve. "It's our weekly date. We always swear before we leave the house that we're going to try something new off the menu, but then we break that swear every time and get our usual order. I get the Indiana Jones and Aria gets the Cancan crepe."

My eyebrows raise. "What's the Cancan crepe look like?"

"It's a bit risqué and it kind of embarrasses me, which is why Aria orders it, I think," says Steve. "It has a leg of chocolate kicking high out of a petticoat of whipped cream over a crepe stuffed with cooked apples and brie."

Steve fumbles somewhat with this description. His embarrassment over this risqué crepe makes me laugh. I look over at him for the first time since Edgar brought our food. I look straight into his eyes, and we laugh together. That was a mistake. I'm stuck here now in his eyes. There's no looking away.

"So, about Vancouver," Steve prompts.

"I need to use the bathroom," I say and launch myself out of my seat and into the restaurant. I'm halfway through the crowded room of people, making a beeline for the back of this place, though I have no idea if that's where the bathroom is, when I run into Edgar's chest. Blind to my stampede through his eatery, Edgar had turned from a customer's table and inadvertently put himself in my path. I bounce off him, but he catches me before I land on a table of people behind me. The Crepes Fairy gives me a perturbed look as he helps to right me. Though I'm back on my feet and stable, he keeps a firm grip on my arms out of concern for the surrounding patrons.

"Bathroom please?" I ask him, intimidated.

"Let me show you where it is," says Edgar. He moves me over a step so I'm a safe distance from any of his customers before letting go of my arms. Edgar then moves past me to take the lead and guide me to the restroom. We walk back toward the wall that starts at the front door. This wall is taken up, end to end, by a long bar with high swivel stools, all filled with people enjoying breakfast. I didn't see this bar when I came in. Edgar turns toward the back wall when we reach the bar. For a fraction of a second, I think to peer over people's shoulders to see what their plates of crepes look like. I quickly push that thought aside, however, and stay focused on following Edgar. When we reach the end of the bar, Edgar stops and turns around so he's looking down into my face.

"There you go," he says.

I look over and see two doors with signs for the bathrooms. The women's bathroom has a girl fairy picture on it and the men's has a boy fairy resembling a young Edgar, pink tutu and all.

"You should go," says Edgar, sounding impatient with me.

I jump a bit at his words and start toward the bathroom door, but then Edgar heaves a large sigh and says, "I meant you should go to Vancouver."

His words stop me. *What did he say?!* asks the Admin. *What business is it of his?*

I look up into Edgar's face and see that he's earnest – impatient with me, but earnest.

"I'm married," I say.

"I know," retorts the Crepes Fairy. "That's a lovely wedding ring you have, and I'm sure Steve has noticed it too. He's not that kind of guy. He's trying to do something nice for you, something good that you are in dire need of, I guess."

"What? What do I need?"

"I have no idea, but if I had to guess I'm going to say you need to relax and do something fun. Life is meant to be enjoyed. An opportunity for a day trip, a small adventure just for you, is sitting outside at your table. This doesn't happen every day. You should go."

"Could you go at a moment's notice? Drop everything?" I gesture around me at his bustling restaurant.

"Yeeesss! I have others in this restaurant working for me who can run things for a day, and I bet you have people in your life who can take over for a day too. Even if I didn't have people to cover for me, I would go. I would kick every one of these folks out and hop on that plane with Steve in a second." Edgar takes a deep breath. "Let me be your fairy spirit guide for the day and give you the best advice I can – go to Vancouver."

I need time to think. Except if I think, then the Admin will take over, and I'll be home in half an hour. The thought of going home makes every muscle in my body seize up. "Okay," I say to Edgar.

"Okay?" he replies. "Okay, you'll go to Vancouver?"

"Yes," I say, with a hint of question in my voice.

You can't! The Admin is yelling over the wall I'm trying to keep her behind.

I understand that I can't, I tell the Admin, *but I think I'm going to anyway.*

"Good," says Edgar. "Now, do you really have to use the bathroom?"

"No. Not really," I admit.

"Then let's get you back to your table." Edgar gestures toward the front door and toward Steve, who I can see is waiting for me. I take a couple steps in that direction. Edgar follows close behind me. I look up and over my shoulder at him.

"Go on," says Edgar. "You can do this, and don't worry about Steve – he's a good man."

When we reach the table, Edgar puts his hands on my shoulders. He talks to Steve over my head. "Steve, Gail has something she'd like to tell you."

"Not a lot of trust here, is there, Edgar?" I ask him.

"Just helping you, dear," replies the Crepe Fairy.

"Edgar is my fairy spirit guide for the day," I tell Steve.

"That's wonderful." Steve grins. He can tell we're going.

I get a gentle squeeze on both shoulders from Edgar, egging me on.

"Steve," I say, "I will go to Vancouver with you today."

Steve's face opens in a wide smile. He claps his hands together and says, "Excellent! I'm glad to hear it. Have a seat and let's finish our breakfast before we get going."

Edgar's hands guide me down into my chair. I look up at him, half of me pleading for more help and the other half saying thank you. The Crepes Fairy smiles down at me, turns to Steve with a smile, and then flits away back into his restaurant.

Steve starts talking about where his plane is waiting and gives me all the logistics of our schedule and our day. His animated chatter helps me ignore the shrieks of the Admin. She gets a word in every few moments, but I choose to stay focused on the good-looking man who is whisking me away for a day. A small thought about John enters the fringe of my mind. I should tell him what I'm doing. This fringe thought really riles the Admin. She sets herself on a rant about how calling my husband should be my priority. I don't want to listen to her. I want to listen to Steve.

CHAPTER 3

*A*fter we finish our crepes and are hugged farewell by our Crepes Fairy, we walk a block back toward Dr. Hu's office and get on Steve's motorcycle. Of course he rides a motorcycle.

The Admin screams bloody murder at me. *You haven't called John yet, and now you're about to get on this death-dealing machine?! John and your boys will never know why Mommy didn't love them enough to stay away from a motorcycle when any time motorcycles are mentioned, you launch into a long tirade about how awful they are!*

She's right. What am I doing? I know what I'm doing. I'm breaking my own rules.

I get on the bike. Steve helps me put a helmet on and then we're off. At first, I squeeze my eyes shut and hold on tight to Steve. I'm as rigid as I can make myself. Maybe if I will myself to be a solid mass, then I won't break when the motorcycle crashes and I'm thrown fifty feet. Then I remember a news report that said when people relax and let themselves bounce during a crash, they aren't hurt as badly. I try to relax, though it isn't easy. I wonder if I open my eyes, will I like what I see and relax a little?

My eyes open to slits, and I see bands of green and light. I open my eyes a bit more and can see the park where I take my kids. It's a school day, so there are just a few parents with toddlers playing in the park. Breezes flow through the trees, and I'm struck by how many trees there are in this park. I've never noticed the trees before, and I've been coming to this park for years. My focus has been on my kids, or my phone, or taken by the Admin keeping me clear on all that must be done when I get home.

I straighten up from my huddle against Steve's back enough that I can shift my head and look around. I see the shops and the coffee place that I frequent. They seem brighter today. The paint on the buildings seems cleaner somehow as they gleam in the sunshine. I see my friend Molly leaving the neighborhood grocery store. I think to wave at her, but there's no way I can release the firm grip I have around Steve's middle. My hands are cemented together at his belly button. I wonder if I'll be able to pry them loose when we stop, or if I'll want to let go.

I take in a sudden and uncomfortable breath at that last adulterous thought. Steve must have felt me tighten up again because I feel one of his hands cover both of mine, giving them a reassuring squeeze. We stop at an intersection, and I hear him call through his helmet that we're not far from the field where he keeps his airplane. What would it be like to be with a man who owns an airplane? Weekend jaunts would be jauntier, I suspect. The last jaunt John and I made was to a drive-in movie in the East Bay. I'd like to say we cuddled in each other's arms and made out, but it was a late-night movie and I fell asleep twenty minutes after the opening credits.

I make an effort to relax and take in this moment. I make my mind notice all the details of where I am. When I think it through, I can't help but giggle. The facts of this moment are that I'm riding with a very handsome man and a large vibrating machine between my legs at the same time. I don't have much choice but to enjoy myself, really. It seems reasonable now that I would have a hard time letting go at the end of our ride.

A few minutes later, we arrive at a small airfield I didn't know existed. I look at the airplanes lined up and ready for flight. The prospect of leaving is now a reality. All of my work tasks come flooding into my head. People are expecting deliverables from me. I should call my manager. I should call John. I should be responsible.

Finally, chides the Admin. *I was thinking you'd completely lost your mind. Now tell this man to take you back.*

"Are you thinking of backing out?" asks Steve. He's parked the motorcycle and has taken off his helmet. I'm still sitting behind him with my helmet on. I guess I haven't moved since we got here.

"I should call and tell someone what I'm doing, like John and my manager at work."

"That's a good idea," says Steve. "Do you think you can do that and not lose steam about going?"

"I don't know," I tell him.

"Okay." Steve doesn't say anything more. He simply sits and waits for me to decide what comes next. I decide to get off the bike and take my helmet off. Steve gets off after me and reaches for my helmet. He stows both mine and his in a compartment on the back end of the bike without speaking. He walks back up the bike and turns to face me. His eyes ask me what I want to do. I still don't know. I don't want to call, and I don't want to leave without calling.

"I'll text them," I announce. The Admin wants to protest, but I've shoved her behind a wall again.

"Sounds good," says Steve. "You text while I prep my plane. It will take me a few minutes and then we'll be on our way."

Thank God for texting. I don't have to worry about how my voice sounds while I lie to my boss or withhold truth from John. I know there isn't a lot of difference between a lie and withholding truth, but in this moment it's a fine line I'm willing to walk. I start the text to my boss. "Family emergency. I need the day off. Sorry, will explain tomorrow."

I don't press send. Can I get away with this? I ask myself.

The Admin has my answer: *You can get away with it. Your boss trusts you because you've been an excellent employee until now. But what does getting away with this make you? It makes you a liar.*

I change the text so it reads 'personal' emergency instead of 'family' emergency.

It's still a lie, scolds the Admin.

It's closer to the truth, I respond.

You'll have to lie tomorrow when your boss asks you what the emergency was. The Admin forever looks ahead.

Yes, I say, *but I'll figure that out later.* I press send. Pressing send is liberating and scary at the same time. Maybe I won't lie tomorrow to cover my tracks and simply claim temporary insanity.

That would be closer to the truth, pipes up the Admin.

I take a couple of deep breaths while I scroll through my contacts for John. I open a text message to him and then my fingers stop. Lying to John, even withholding the truth, is not something I've done before, not on this scale anyway. There's been the occasional white lie to save his feelings, a faked orgasm or two, pretending to listen attentively as he rambles on about the mechanical system he's currently designing for either himself or for a contract. This is bigger. It will hurt him if I lie about flying off with a handsome stranger.

Don't do this to him, says the Admin. *John will think you don't love him anymore. He'll think you're looking for something or someone else.*

I am looking for something else. Wait. That doesn't sound right. I want John, I think, but if I tell him what I'm doing I'll end up talking myself out of this trip.

Yes, the Admin agrees, *you should be talking yourself out of this for your husband and for the sake of your marriage. Did you just say you think you want John?*

I'm saying that I'm doing this for me.

Selfish, rules the Admin. *You're taking too much from others to do this just for you.*

Maybe, but I should get to do something for me. I want to do this. I want to see Vancouver with Steve. I don't want to hurt my husband. I start the text message to John. "I'm doing something for me today. I'll fill you in later. I'll be back in time to get the kids."

I look at the text. It's the truth. I press send. This time, pressing send doesn't feel liberating or scary. It feels sad.

I look up at Steve, who is walking around the nose of his plane talking with another man carrying a clipboard. They speak for a few seconds more, then the clipboard man walks away. Steve looks at me and waves me over. "We're good to go," he calls.

I nod to him and start to turn off my phone and put it away. Just then I get a reply text from John. It says, "Good for you. Have fun."

I take a deep breath in and stow my phone in my purse. As I reach Steve he asks me, "Everything okay?"

"I hope so" is my response and my prayer. "Let's go."

CHAPTER 4

I have that feeling I get every time I sit in a roller coaster that hasn't started moving yet. The bar is down and the attendants are standing back from the connected cars. They signal the operator that all is clear and the ride can begin. Steve's airplane does a slow taxi into position at the end of a runway that looks shorter than I expected. I have a sudden need to use the bathroom. I remind myself that I get that urge at the start of roller coaster rides too, and it will pass. Either that or I'm about to make a mess.

Everything is loud. I look at Steve as he checks gauges and flips toggles, and he is calm. He looks like he's about to drive off in a car, except the steering wheel looks like it belongs on a video game and it isn't shaped like a wheel. I wonder what it's called if it isn't called a steering wheel. There's one in front of me too. I very much want to be in a back passenger seat now. I'm afraid I might touch the steering thing in front of me and cause a fiery crash. My hands fly down to the sides of my seat cushion and squeeze hard, just as the plane accelerates down the runway. The ride has started. My stomach clenches. Instead of a slow ascent up a steep hill, we're screaming toward the end of our runway. A grassy field waits at the end, and I'm certain it will flip this plane if we hit it. We go faster and faster to the very end, when the plane leaves the runway and starts its slow climb up a steep hill of air. As soon as we leave the ground, the speed of the plane doesn't feel strained. In fact, the plane seems to calm down around me as it settles into flight, and so do I. The difference between Steve's plane moving on the ground and moving in the air is profound, and comforting. My hands loosen their grip from the sides of my seat and find their way back into my lap. All those times I looked up and wished to be on a plane and here I am. I hope someone is looking up at this little plane and making a wish that comes true someday.

We sit in silence for the first few minutes of the flight. I watch my city disappear and wonder how far we'll go before I cease to recognize the landscape. I don't think it will be much further. The thought of seeing new landscapes from high in the air makes me giddy.

"What do you think?" I hear Steve ask me over our headsets.

"I think I'm on a magic carpet flying away." I'm almost singing as I speak. "Thank you."

"You're welcome," says Steve. "Enjoy the flight – it's a beautiful ride."

"This is so much fun. I can't remember now why it was so hard for me to say yes to this. I would much rather be sitting here than at work. I don't like my job." I can hear the Admin grunt from the back of my brain. I'm holding her at bay, but negative talk of work fuels her.

"Why?" asks Steve.

"It doesn't interest me." It's both easy and hard to admit this. The job is more than I deserve. "The people I work with are fantastic, the pay is high, the benefits are off-the-chart amazing. I'm acknowledged all the time, people telling me how good I am at my job. I'm even about to be promoted." The Admin settles. I look over at Steve, who looks impressed with me. "I'm going to be a manager."

"You don't look happy about it," says Steve.

I shrug my shoulders. "It's professional development," I say. "I've applied to other jobs to see if a change will help, but the positions I've applied for usually need me to have management experience. I've never managed people before, so this will be a good step forward."

25

"You're not happy there but you think it's good for you to be there because it's good for your résumé?"

"I'm supporting my family and growing as a professional. I'm grateful for that." A morose chuckle escapes me after I speak these words. Steve glances over to see what's going on with me.

"Is something funny?" he asks.

"No, that's the trouble. The work I do wasn't that fun to begin with, and it's less so each year. At best, it can be interesting. The interesting days help. I work with a team of analysts and engineers to run tests on how one brand of software or hardware outperforms the competition, or doesn't. We bring all the data together, and I compile it into a final analysis that the team signs off on. Then I write an article based on the analysis that is published and consumed worldwide. I do like that part. I like knowing that something I've written is helping people in Sweden or Brazil or Japan."

"My coworkers talk seriously about this stuff all the time in meetings and in the hallway, and I just stand there wishing I was anywhere else. I don't want to hear about software anymore. I don't want to speak that language anymore. I zero in on my tasks and do my job. I make sure to do a good job too. I don't want to let my coworkers down, and I don't want to get fired. I feel like a whiny brat saying all this. There's so much going right for me, and I wish I wasn't there." I do feel whiny, and I feel relieved. Someone other than the Admin knows how I feel.

"I can see how some people would tell you to count your blessings and stop whining," says Steve. I know he's right. I nod my head that I agree. "But I'm not one of those people. Find what you love to do and do that."

I balk. "You make it sound easy. I guess your job is a joy that you were always good at and were paid for since the day you started? Is it a daily thrill that never feels like work?"

"My job developed out of a designing hobby I had. Apps became an easy medium, yes, but it hasn't been easy lately. I've been stuck, for a long time, and have had to take smaller jobs assisting others."

"What do you mean stuck? How are you stuck?" I ask.

"I can't think of anything that I want to design, and I can't find a contract that I'm excited to work on."

"Why do you think you're stuck?"

Steve takes a long pause as he thinks through my question. I'm not sure he's going to answer it at all, which suits me. I'm pretty done with this conversation. Then he says, "I'm not saying you can find and start a new paying career today or tomorrow, but you can change the course of your life with a single choice. It just takes a decision and a commitment to it."

"It's not as easy as that."

Just then the plane sputters like it's running out of gas. Steve starts making some quick moves. He checks dials and flips switches in rapid-fire motion.

"What's happening?" I ask. I try to keep my voice calm while Steve's calm starts to waver.

"An engine is shutting down," Steve tells me.

"Why?"

"I don't know why, but we have to land."

"Land?" My voice cracks and squeaks. "Where can we land? Are we going to crash?"

"The plane is steady enough that I can keep us level. We'll land fine, just not where we thought we would," says Steve.

"Oh, my God. Oh, my God." My hands grip my knees hard. My eyes are wide and glued to what's coming. I want to shut my eyes or look away, but my eyes and my mind won't let me. I don't know what to do.

I told you what to do. The Admin is just as panicked as me. *I told you not to get on this plane, and now we're going die – just like I said we would!*

"I'm going to set down on that road," says Steve.

I see the road. It's narrow but paved. Steve lines up the plane with the road. Terrible sounds ring loud in my ears – battle noises from the remaining engine fighting to keep itself and us alive, keep the plane on target. I hear fists of air pummeling the plane outside. The walls seem thin as they rattle against the wind. Getting closer and closer to ground, time seems to slow. I don't want time to slow down this much. I try to breathe to keep pace with my heart, but my breath has stopped in my throat. The slow motion is awful. It gives me time to memorize the color of the road, the shape of the plane's nose, the fields of wildflowers that bank the road. These are my last memories, the last things I'll see. I think of my kids. I want their faces to be in my head. I think of John. The road is getting closer – too close, too fast.

Then it happens. The wheels touch the ground, and we bounce. The plane skips up from the road. I suck in air and grip my knees even harder. The tires touch again and remain on the road this time. I hear them screaming. The rubber of the tires must be peeling from them like skin on the road. I start screaming. I wish I'd started sooner. My screaming drowns out the sounds around me.

We're slowing down. I watch as Steve holds onto the steering wheel hard while the plane slows itself and comes to a stop. He flips switches again in rapid fire. Watching him distracts me from my screaming. I stop in time to hear the sounds of the battle in the remaining engine quiet and disappear. Steve looks out his window then checks gauges. "There's no fire in the downed engine," he tells me. "We're okay."

We sit still in our chairs. We look straight ahead, and breathe. Time passes while we sit there. I don't know how long. The Admin takes over as I struggle to reboot my mind. *Look around you and figure out where you are,* she tells me.

I steal glances through the window to my side, then through the windshield where the road stretches ahead of us, then over to Steve. Steve has bent his head back into his headrest. His eyes are closed, and he's breathing hard. I'm not able to speak yet, so I continue to look around. The world around me looks the same as it did before our emergency detour. Everything looks the same, but I am not the same.

Are you hurt? asks the Admin.

My knees hurt. I look down into my lap. I see the iron grip of my hands on my knees. The grip feels permanent. My fingers are straps of steel affixed around and over my kneecaps. I tell myself to let go, but it doesn't work. I concentrate. I can feel my fingers, but they refuse to release their grip.

"I'm going to come around to your side of the plane," says Steve. He exits out the door on his side and comes around to my door. He opens it and a rush of hot air enters the plane, suffocating my already staggered breathing. Steve starts talking to me. "Well, that was unexpected" – he removes my headset – "but we made it down intact, including the plane, which is great. Do you want to get out of the plane?"

I nod yes. I don't move.

"Are you feeling stuck in your seat?"

I nod yes again, and I start to cry.

"Okay," says Steve. "I'm going to unbuckle you." He releases the buckle from its clip but can't get the strap past my arms. "Can you let go of your knees, please?"

I shake my head no.

"Right. I'm going to see if I can help you so you can get out of the plane, okay?"

I nod yes. Tears stream down my face. I'm silent, however, strangely mute. The part of my brain that makes sound hasn't come back online yet.

Let him help you, instructs the Admin, *then we'll figure out what needs to happen next.*

I watch his fingers gently pry my right hand free and then hold it. He does the same for my left hand. I watch as he rubs my hands with his thumbs to soothe them, and me. After a few seconds, I look up into his face.

"Ready to come back to Earth?" He's making a joke. I don't think it's funny. I shoot a look of hurt and blame at him. Steve looks as though I slapped him.

"How am I supposed to get home now?" Reboot complete, I'm talking.

Yes! says the Admin, *keep talking!*

"What?"

"You said I'd be back in time to pick my kids up from school. How is that going to happen?"

"I really don't think that's what is important right now," says Steve.

29

"It's important to me!" I yell at him. I move to get out of the plane. Another milestone, I'm moving. Steve is still holding my hands and helps me down. He doesn't let go of my hands.

"What do we do now, Steve?!"

"Gail, we just survived an emergency landing of a small aircraft." He's half-screaming at me now. I can see he's trying to compose himself, but it isn't working. "We're breathing air and standing on our feet. We were able to leave the downed plane without digging ourselves out of its wreckage. This is a happy moment, and you're missing it!" He's full-on screaming. Not such a happy moment after all. "You will get back to your kids as a whole person. I think they'll forgive you if you're a little late today."

"Fine!" I scream back at him. "I'm happy I'm alive!"

"Good!" he screams back.

"I think you should let go of my hands now!" I yell. Steve looks down at our hands. It surprises him to see we're connected. He takes a breath and lets me go. He continues to look down and takes a couple more ragged breaths to calm himself. Then he starts to move back around the plane to his door. He gets in the plane and uses the radio to call for help.

"Mayday, Mayday, this is plane 4770 out of San Francisco, was heading to Vancouver. I've made an emergency landing about fifty miles north of the Oregon border. Can anyone hear me?" I hold my breath, wishing hard that someone will respond.

"Plane 4770, this is Sheriff Tracy Burnham of the township of New Hope. What is your condition?" Her country voice is the sweetest sound I think I've ever heard.

"I and my one passenger are not hurt," Steve reports. "I was able to land my plane safely on a road. An engine died, so I landed immediately. I'm looking at my GPS, and it says I'm on a stretch of Route 9 east of town."

"Good for you, plane 4770. I am going to get on Route 9 to find you and your passenger. Do you have flares to place on the road both in front of and behind your aircraft?"

"I do," Steve answers her.

"Good, you do that and sit tight for my arrival. What are your names?" Sheriff Burnham asks.

"I'm Steve Wright," he replies. This is the first time I've heard his last name. I got into a plane to go on a trip with a man to another country, and I didn't know his last name. "And I'm here with Gail... hold on. What's your last name, Gail?"

"Harker. I'm Gail Harker." Nice to meet you, Steve Wright, I think to myself.

"Gail Harker is my passenger," Steve tells the sheriff over the radio.

"Okay, Steve, you and Gail stick close to the airplane, and I'll be there before you know it. Sheriff Burnham out."

"Thank you, Sheriff, plane 4770 out." Steve rummages behind the pilot seat and brings out two flares. He works silently. I walk to the side of the road and sit with my back to the plane. I look out into a field of flowers and grass and trees. I try to focus my mind on the beautiful landscape as I hear Steve light the flares. The smell of smoke and burning chemicals from the flares against the lovely, lonely scene in front of me seems to capture how I feel. I should be out in the meadow picking flowers, happy to be alive. Instead, I feel a slow, bright burn of hurt and fear inside me. The Admin takes a seat next to me. She doesn't speak just yet. She doesn't have to.

This is where adventure leads, I say to her.

It's what you've known all along, confirms the Admin.

I broke the rules to try and have some fun today.

Then, WHAM, you got hit with calamity. It's the price you pay for selfish fun.

The Admin is right.

Steve sits down on the other side of me. "I'm glad you're here," he says.

The Admin and I both whip our heads round to look at him. Words fail us.

"I'm not saying I'm glad you almost crashed in my plane with me," Steve explains. "I'm saying I'm glad you're here on this trip with me."

Seriously, this man isn't right. You should have listened to me, goads the Admin.

"I still think we should go to Vancouver," Steve announces.

He's insane! I've been saying this all along, and now here's the proof, says the Admin.

"Hear me out," says Steve. "There's still a journey out here for us today."

Journey over, says the Admin. *He nearly killed you in a plane – as you predicted, if you recall. It's time to turn back.*

"I don't know how we're going to get there," Steve continues.

I don't know how you're going to explain all this to John, says the Admin.

"But I think we should keep going. Maybe my plane isn't the magic carpet. Maybe it brought us to the magic carpet hangar we were meant to find. Our next magic carpet may be right around the corner."

And maybe that one will crash too! the Admin is shouting at Steve. *You're on drugs, aren't you?*

"You promised you would get me home in time to pick up my kids. We came close to dying a few minutes ago. Now you want to forget home and go to Vancouver still?" Steve doesn't answer. I turn my body so I'm facing him better, putting my back to the Admin for a moment.

I look into Steve's eyes. "Why are you doing this?" I ask.

Steve takes a deep breath and looks out into the field. He's silent for a moment, considering my question, I expect. "I don't believe in coincidence. I don't think it was coincidence that we met this morning and now we're fifty miles into Oregon. I want to see what happens next," he says.

"Is that it? It sounds like you're watching a movie. This is my life."

"It's my life too. I'm on this journey with you for a reason."

"What reason?"

"I need to figure out what happens next with me. I think that's why I'm here. I wanted to do something for me today and now I'm here. I've been concentrating on Aria and trying to make our lives normal again for a long while. I can't remember when I last did something that was just for me. I want to see what happens next," he says. "Don't you?"

"What do mean about making your lives normal again?" I ask him. "Are you divorced? Because I think that's where I'm heading if I keep going north with you, Steve. I'm not sure how I'm going to explain almost dying in a plane crash to John and then tell him that I decided to pick myself up and keep traveling with you instead of going home."

"My wife died."

I stare at Steve. I think I stop breathing.

"Aria's mom, my wife, she died. It was unexpected. I don't have anyone I can blame, not even her, that she isn't here anymore. She walked out our door to go to work one morning, and then she was gone." Steve stops talking. Maybe he's waiting for me to say something. I can only sit and stare at a pain I can't imagine.

"Most people ask me how it happened," Steve says. I nod to him, which he takes as a sign to keep talking. "She had an aneurysm. She died instantly. She was riding a bus to work. It seems unreal that a person can be taken so easily. One minute she's there and the next she's gone."

"What was her name?" I ask him.

"Anabeth."

"That's a pretty name."

"Yes, it is. She was a pretty woman too. You can really tell how pretty she was by looking at Aria." Steve's voice breaks. The sorrow in his face melts into fear, and his voice becomes a whisper. "It scares me how much they look alike. I'm afraid it will happen to Aria. I've asked a dozen doctors if getting an aneurysm is hereditary, and they all say no. Still, it scares me that I could lose her too." Steve is crying now. He bows his head into his left hand and lets himself cry.

I scoot myself closer to him and put both my arms around him. His right hand reaches up and squeezes my arm, while his left covers his face. Watching Steve's grief and fear over this traumatic loss makes me think of John. Life without John is something I can't fathom. I can't say I haven't considered divorce during our more trying times, but divorce and death are different. My life and my boys' lives work with John in it. Then I connect the dots. I nearly did that to John. I almost died in a plane crash. My own wellspring of tears flows again. The first torrent came from my own near-death shock; now this river is for John, and for Steve.

Time passes and the crying slows for us both. Steve's left hand drops from his face. His right still has a hold of my arm. I rest my head on his shoulder.

"Today is important to me," says Steve. "I didn't get how important until it looked like this stop outside the town of New Hope might be the end of it. I don't want to escape my life. Today isn't that for me. I am glad to get a break from it, though."

"I understand," I tell him.

"I want to get back to Aria, and I want you to get back to your family. Right here and now, even though my plane died and we survived an emergency landing, I'm glad I'm here, and I'm glad you're here too, and I want to see what happens next." Steve shifts so he can look straight at my face. I lift my head and look up at him. "What do you think?" he asks me.

I don't have time to answer. What happens next pulls up in her squad car.

CHAPTER 5

Sheriff Burnham pulls up a few feet from where we sit at the side of the road. "How you folks doing?" she calls to us as she gets out of her car. Her Stetson hat, brown uniform, and tan tie accentuate the no-nonsense stance she takes as she surveys the scene. The sheriff glances to the plane and the lit flares. She sees Steve has done well. Then Sheriff Burnham puts her focus back on us sitting by the side of the road. When her eyes rest on us, I realize that my arms are still around Steve. I straighten up and loosen my hug. As I do, Steve gives my arm a last squeeze and drops his hand. I see the sheriff's sympathetic reaction to our red eyes. Our sheriff has a kind face.

"Hi, Sheriff Burnham," says Steve. "Thank you so much for coming to our rescue." Steve moves to stand, and I follow him to my feet.

"Happy to help," Sheriff Burnham responds, "and please call me Sheriff Tracy, or just Sheriff is fine. You look a bit shaken. Are you doing okay?"

"I am," says Steve. "I think we both just had some post-emergency-landing emotion to get out."

"Surely," says Sheriff Tracy.

"This is my friend Gail."

"Hi, Sheriff Tracy." I wave to her.

"Hi there, Gail, and how are you doing?" The sheriff's eyes assess me while she waits for my answer. I get the feeling she doesn't miss anything, so the truth is best. I think about what to say. During my pause, Steve turns to look at me, curious about the answer himself, I suspect.

I think it through, and when I'm sure of my answer, I say, "I believe I'm doing well, all things considered. Thanks, Sheriff."

"Glad to hear it," says Sheriff Tracy. Steve smiles at me. He's glad to hear it too. "Well, then, I guess the first order of business is to take care of your plane," says the sheriff. "On the way over, I had our dispatch call the man who flies the US Mail out of Portland to all of us in this area. He knows his way around a plane's engine. I hope you don't mind. Dispatch got hold of him, so he's on his way now."

"I don't mind," says Steve. "Thank you."

"Surely," replies the sheriff. "So you folks were heading to Vancouver, you said? Heading up for the Celebration of Light then."

"Celebration of Light?" I ask.

"Yes, Vancouver's biggest festival of the year. You mean you folks were flying into Vancouver, and you didn't know the Celebration of Light is about to start? Tonight is the first night of the competition.""The celebration is a competition?" asks Steve, looking as clueless as I am.

"That's right," says Sheriff Tracy. She regards us to see if we're serious in our lack of knowledge. When she sees that we are, she looks flummoxed. "It's an international competition where three countries compete within a few nights of one another for who has the best fireworks show."

"A fireworks competition." Steve is impressed. "Now that sounds fun."

"Oh, it's beautiful and exciting and fun! My husband, Henry, and I have been going for the last five years running. We love it. We'd be there now except two days ago Henry slipped on some wet pavement and ruptured a disc in his back, so we aren't going to make it." There's some thick regret in her voice. "The two of you are going to

Vancouver during a busy time. I'm not sure how you'll make it now, of course."

We each look over at the downed plane. I'm still not sure what I want to do – follow the yellow brick road or click my heels and go home – but not having options in this moment helps to keep that decision, and the Admin, at bay.

Sounds of an approaching vehicle rumble behind us. We turn in unison to see a rather worn blue-green truck in the distance. "Ah, that'll be Ned," says the sheriff. "Ned's a good egg. Pretty smart when it comes to airplanes. Pretty smart when it comes to lots of things, really. He used to work at Boeing as a plane mechanic. He's been running mail for a few years now."

When Ned emerges from his truck, I see a handsome man in his fifties who could be Sam Elliott's brother. I've always had a soft spot for Sam Elliott. I don't care that he's thirty years older than me.

"Heya, Ned," shouts the sheriff as Ned approaches.

"Sheriff" is Ned's reply.

"Ned, we have Gail here, and this is Steve. Steve is the pilot."

Ned bobs his chin up slightly, indicating his hello to us. "Come take a look at her, Ned," and the sheriff waves Ned over to our plane.

"It's the pilot-side engine, Ned," says Steve, who walks over to Ned, shakes his hand, and then leads him to the plane. "I'm very glad you're here to take a look. Thank you for coming out."

"Yeah," utters Ned who doesn't appear to be much of a talker. He and Steve walk around to look at the troubled engine while Sheriff Tracy and I hang back and let them work.

"Ned'll get it figured out soon enough," says Sheriff Tracy. I smile in response. "Have the two of you been friends long?" she asks me.

I look at my watch and see that it's 10:30 a.m. "I have known Steve for a little over two hours."

"Really?" asks the sheriff. Her eyes narrow a bit. "Is there some sort of emergency in Vancouver this stranger is helping you get to?"

"No," I say. "No emergency. This all just happened. We met in our dentist's office. He took me to breakfast and offered to fly me to Vancouver because I've never seen it before. I wanted something different to happen today, and this small outing presented itself." I can hear how strange this sounds.

"Uh-huh." Sheriff Tracy's eyes narrow as she regards my story. She can see there's more to it. "Well, he is a nice-looking man."

"I'm married. I'm not here to cheat on my husband. It isn't like that. And I'm not running away from anything either. My marriage is working, and I have a good life." I rush to get these words out, hoping she will understand my motives. I feel compelled to prove my innocence against the doubting stare of this sheriff. I can tell she's not satisfied that she's been told everything.

"Why did you want something different to happen today?" she asks.

"I'm still trying to figure that out."

"I know this may be a very prying question, especially since I'm a sheriff standing here in my uniform, but is something or someone hurting you?"

"No," I tell her. "No one is hurting me, but I hurt anyway." Whoa. Did I just say that? I did and it's true. I hurt. I've been hurting for a while. I must have ignored it. The hurt is real but it's still news to me, and there's more to say. I can feel the words bubbling to the surface. Sheriff Tracy sees the words are coming and waits patiently. "I look at my life and I see so much that I love, so much that I'm grateful for, but I don't see me."

"There it is," she says. "Okay. Can you see yourself now? Now that you've done something different today?"

I let out a long breath that is almost a whistle. "All I see is me right now, and I don't like what I see. I took this stupid risk that led to a near-death crash in an airplane. It's like I've rubber-banded to another extreme."

"It isn't stupid to take a risk, especially if it's a risk on you," she says. "Sounds like you gave yourself a good dose of you today – something you've needed for a while. What's more, the day's just started." A wide smile spreads across her face. I'm not sure what to make of it. I hear Steve and Ned walking toward us.

"Ned can fix the engine," says Steve, "but it'll take him most of today. He says he can get the part he needs when he flies to Portland soon for the mail."

"Where is Ned going to fix your plane?" I ask Steve. It seems outrageous to me that Steve's plane, along with the two of us, are going to sit on this road waiting for Ned to fly to Portland and back.

"Ned says he has a lot of space on his property where he has his workshop. He even brought a tow bar with him, and he's going to tow my plane back to his place now."

"Well, that's perfect!" Sheriff Tracy is nearly shouting. She looks ecstatic, and I have no idea why. "Ned, after you tow his plane, get Lucy ready. I'll bring these two out in about forty-five minutes to meet you at your field. You're going to take them with you to Portland."

" 'Kay" is Ned's syllabic response before he starts walking to his truck.

"PORTLAND?" the Admin and I exclaim in unison.

"I'll explain in the car. We have to hurry so we have time to make a stop before you get going with Ned," says the sheriff before she turns and practically sprints to her car. Steve and I haven't moved from where we stand. The sheriff looks over her shoulder and waves to us. "Come on, you two! You've gotten yourselves this far today – now it's time to get moving again." Steve and I look at each other. Neither of us is certain of what we should do.

"Please trust me," says the sheriff. "It's no coincidence that you landed on my road in my town. I can tell you don't know what to do next, so you have to trust me now that I know." She's hopping with excitement. "Please just get in the car."

Sheriff Tracy opens her driver-side door and beams a smile at us as she bounces into her seat. Steve and I look at each other with the same question in our eyes for the other: are you going with her? Steve nods yes and starts walking to the car. The Admin tells me no, but I counter her, asking if she'd rather I sat at the side of this road alone waiting for the others to get back. *Yes*, she says, which is enough to make me walk over and get in the car.

CHAPTER 6

Five minutes down the road, Sheriff Tracy turns right onto a dirt path. Ahead of us is a huge, purple barn. The barn has these words painted on its side in tall, white lettering:

GIUSEPPE AND JULIETTE'S CIRCUS TRAINING

Where YOU are the greatest show on earth!

A great sense of foreboding washes over me. I can't imagine I'm going to like what comes next: lion-taming? swallowing swords? Sheriff Tracy pulls up to the front door of the barn and stops the car. A small woman with short brown hair comes out the front door of the barn to greet us. She looks Mediterranean with her gorgeous olive skin, and she doesn't look much older than me.

"Juliette!" says Sheriff Tracy as she parks and then jumps out of the car.

"Hi, Sheriff, you're early," says Juliette. "Everything okay?"

"Everything is great! This here is Gail and Steve." Sheriff Tracy looks back to see we're still sitting in the car. "Come on, you two, come meet Juliette!"

I let out an 'I can't believe this is happening to me' sigh and open my door. Steve follows suit, though he skips the dramatic sigh.

"Juliette, these two are passing through on their way to Vancouver. I don't have time to explain, but they're on a journey and it's brought them here to us for a short time. I want to get these two flying through the air for just a couple of passes each before I get them over to Ned. He's flying them to Portland soon in Lucy. Is Giuseppe here?"

"He's here," says Juliette. She looks at us and a grin spreads over her face.

"Well, let's get him," says Sheriff Tracy. "We don't have much time!" Sheriff Tracy races into the barn and shouts for Giuseppe.

"Have either of you ever swung on a trapeze before?" asks Juliette.

I hear Juliette ask this question, and then the strangest thing happens. Steve, who is standing right next to me, sounds very far away when he responds to Juliette. He's talking to her, saying something like, "a trapeze? No! I've never been on a trapeze…" and on he goes. He sounds excited. I strain to hear him. I see Juliette motion to an area behind the barn. She turns and walks in that direction. Without asking them to, my feet start walking to follow her. I'm not sure I want them to, but my feet carry me along the front of the barn, straight around the corner, to the open field behind it.

A circus ring is planted in the ground, filled in with sand. A trapeze looms inside it. Though I know it isn't possible, it looks about the size of Mount Everest to me. Only a barn could hide something this big and imposing. This trapeze mountain stands at the ready for those brave enough to spurn nature and dare to fly.

I am not such a person.

My ears feel like they are burning. I reach up and cup my hands around them, and they do indeed feel hot to my touch. I hear someone talking next to me, but the words are muffled. Something is wrong with me. I feel a hand on my shoulder. I look over and see it's Steve. He looks concerned. He's saying something to me, but I can't make it out. I see his hands move slowly to my face and I wonder what he's doing. Then I feel his hands on my hands, taking them away from my ears.

"Gail, are you okay? Is something wrong with your ears?" Steve asks me.

"They're hot," I explain.

"Your whole head is red like a beet," Juliette tells me. "It's nerves. You're just nervous. Don't worry, it happens to a lot of people. Blood has rushed to your head. That's why your ears are hot. You may feel a bit light-headed, too, but that'll pass."

"It will?" I ask her. "You've seen this happen before?"

"I see this all the time. Even seasoned pros get rushes of nerves every now and then." Juliette is trying to reassure me, but it's not working.

Sheriff Tracy appears from around the barn with a man in a bright blue unitard and black ballet slippers. Normally, I would have giggled at the sight of him, but his uniform makes my heart sink to around my belly button. This is happening. Sheriff Tracy is so excited she's glowing. The sheriff reaches down and starts to unbuckle her police pants. Half a second later, her pants are down around her ankles and she's stepping out of them. I start to look away, but my eyes are shocked into attention at seeing the bright pink fabric covering her legs. Sheriff Tracy is wearing a unitard under her uniform. She came prepared.

"I wear my costume to save time when I get here. It's such a pain to get it on and off – much easier just to keep it on under my clothes." Though this explanation from Sheriff Tracy makes sense, the look of bewilderment doesn't leave my face. I don't know where to look to make sense of what's happening. I look to Steve. He has his arms crossed tight across his chest. His fists are buried somewhere up in his armpits. He's nervous too. He sees me looking over at him and gives me a smile that is nervous, but also excited. It's a 'what the heck – why not try?' kind of smile that makes the heart behind my belly button throb.

Juliette, Sheriff Tracy, and Giuseppe walk toward me. It feels like they're closing ranks around me. I have a fight-or-flight moment but somehow hold myself together enough to stand my ground. I throw my hands up in front of me – palms out – and shout, "Stop!" They stop. "I don't think I can do this. I'm sorry. I have a fear of falling. This is too much. I'll just watch." I'm rambling.

Sheriff Tracy walks toward me again, but slowly. I stand my ground. My hands are still up in front of me. I tell her, "It's okay. It's okay. It looks like fun, for you. I can't wait to see you do this."

The sheriff reaches out carefully and takes my left hand in hers. She doesn't speak. She looks at me with the kindest eyes I can ever remember seeing. She looks at me without speaking for a long moment. I see her take a big breath in through her nose. Instinctively, I do the same. She blows the air out through her mouth, and so do I. She smiles at me. I try to smile back, but it's a failed attempt.

"This is the easiest thing you'll ever do, Gail. That's how it frees you, because it's so darn easy to hang on to a bar while gravity takes you for a ride. All your ideas around what makes this hard are just ideas. You can do this."

Sheriff Tracy gives my hand a small tug and starts us walking to the trapeze. I shake my head no, but my feet betray me again and move me forward. Sheriff Tracy doesn't break eye contact with me, and she keeps talking, which distracts me from the ongoing mutiny below my ankles. "I'm going to talk you through what we're doing at every step. It's simple as pie. First, we're going to put some gloves on your hands." I feel another hand take my right hand from where it's still outstretched in front of me. I see in my periphery that it's Juliette. I don't take my eyes off my sheriff, however. I can feel Juliette put a glove on my hand. She gives the other glove to Sheriff Tracy. Juliette holds my right hand in hers as we all continue to walk together.

"It's a safe ride," says Sheriff Tracy. She glances down to my hand that she's holding so she can work the glove on. My eyes follow, and I see the white leather glove go over my fingers. My fingers stick out where the glove ends at my knuckles. I wiggle them a bit. "The gloves are fingerless because they're meant to keep the sweat off your palms while you're holding the bar. Having your fingers free helps you grip the bar." Sheriff Tracy sounds like she's talking to a kindergartner. I'm not mad. I don't think I could comprehend adult-speak right now. We've stopped walking. We're at the foot of a ladder. I look up the ladder and feel my heart leap from behind my belly button straight up into my throat.

"Here's why it's safe." Sheriff Tracy is talking again. "When we get to that platform up there, Giuseppe and Juliette are going to put a harness around your waist. The harness has multiple failsafe hitches. You cannot tumble out of bounds of the net in any way. Plus, you see how wide the net is – it stretches wide in every direction, so it'll catch you no matter what." I look at the expanse of net that stretches long and wide before me, and it does seem vast from this angle.

"Now we climb the ladder," Sheriff Tracy says to me. I look up the ladder and am unable to see the top. It seems to stretch on forever. Giuseppe leaps to the third rung right in front of my eyes and starts climbing. I watch him for two seconds then look back to Sheriff Tracy. I look to her for help.

Sheriff Tracy reaches up and touches my cheek with her fingers. "Let your ideas of fear and reasoning go, Gail, because they are just ideas. You don't know what's going to happen until you put yourself up there and let it happen. Climb the ladder. I'll be right behind you."

The Admin peels back the viscous layer of dread stinting my brain activity to state with clear sincerity, *You walked away from a near-death event. Do not tempt the Grim Reaper again.*

I take a deep breath. I look up the long ladder. I whimper out to the small crowd around me, "People die doing this."

Juliette puts her arms around my waist and speaks soft words in my ear. "People die when there is no net, or no harness, or no one around spotting them. You will be as safe up there in the harness, over the net, with Giuseppe and I looking after you, as you are here on the ground in my arms."

I look at the ladder rung directly in front of my face. Juliette releases me and grabs that very rung and starts to climb. She's leading me up.

You don't ride roller coasters anymore, you stay out of the fast lane on highways, you've learned the safer seats to be in when riding a train or flying in an airplane because you know it's your duty as a wife and mother to avoid any risk of death. Don't do this, demands the Admin.

You're right, I respond, *I have been that person. Today I've been someone who rides on a motorcycle and takes jaunts in a small aircraft. Why can't I be a person brave enough to try this too?*

I tell my hands to grip the rung in front of me and I tell my feet to start climbing. It's an odd kind of comfort, to feel that my feet and I are working together again. I climb. I keep my eyes on each rung as it appears in front of me, and I climb. I wish I could leave the Admin on the ground, but she is on my back and sticking with me. The whole situation is enough to overpower me and cause me to stop breathing, yet my breathing continues. In fact, I'm acutely aware of my breathing. I hear my breath as it gets louder and more labored – sharp sucks in that lead to jagged gusts out. In and out, reach and climb. I find my way to the platform without thinking about it. My mind was on my breath.

Giuseppe stretches his hand out to me as I reach the platform. I reach up for his hand. He grabs mine firmly and practically lifts me to the platform in one deft upward movement of his arm. I land on the platform. His hand leaves mine and moves around my waist before I can blink. He has a solid hold on me that I innately trust. He shifts me over a few inches so that Sheriff Tracy can join us on the platform. I look around for Steve, but he doesn't appear. I look down the ladder a bit to see how close he is to the platform and don't see him. It isn't until I look farther over the platform that I see he's still on the ground. I can't believe he didn't come up with me, and I can't believe how far away he looks down on the ground.

"It's my turn next," Steve shouts up at me. He even has the gall to give me a thumbs-up.

"He better take a turn," I whisper aloud, "or I'll find something to beat him with, like a lion-tamer's whip." The other three on the platform laugh at this. Juliette and Giuseppe have started putting the harness on me. I'm impressed with how they're doing this since Giuseppe's grip around my middle still feels solid. Sheriff Tracy, meanwhile, is dipping her hands one at a time into a bucket strapped to a pole at the side of the platform. Her hands emerge coated in white chalk that she spreads evenly all over them. She rubs and then claps her hands together hard.

"I'm going to take the first pass," Sheriff Tracy says to me. "Watch what I do. When it's your turn, you'll do the exact same thing. I'm going to swing out once and come back, then swing out again to halfway and let go of the bar. I'm going to keep myself flat like paper when I fall, so I'm on my back when the net catches me."

"It doesn't make sense," I say to her. Sheriff Tracy takes my statement in and thinks it through.

"I know," she says. "It goes against all of what your mind and body thinks is right for you to do, but those are just ideas, remember? Know that you're safe. Know that you're with the right people in this moment. What you can't know is what happens next until you let it happen. You can't know what this will mean to you until you've tried."

With that, Giuseppe hands Sheriff Tracy the bar. She grips it with her left hand while her right holds a vertical pole. She centers herself so she's faced forward. I see her lean back and rise up on her toes. Then, in one graceful motion, she grabs the bar with both hands, hops up into the air, and flies. She flies right before my eyes. It's beautiful to watch her. I see her body move through the air to the other end of the trapeze structure, then I see it glide back toward us. It's as though she's riding a very large swing. Once again, her body moves away from us. Halfway across the trapeze field, I hear Giuseppe make a loud and sharp yell, *Hup!* On cue, as soon as the *hup* is spoken, Sheriff Tracy lets go of the bar and falls. She falls and the net catches her, just like she said it would.

The net bounces her up and, in mid-air, I see her right herself into a standing position. The next time she touches the net, she's on her feet. She walks to the side of the net and grabs its edge. I see her roll over the side of the net in a smooth somersault dismount, dangle for a moment, then release her hold and land on the ground with no trouble at all.

"That was incredible," I say aloud.

"Now it's your turn," Juliette says to me. "It can be as easy as she just made it look, if you let it be. Turn off your brain. Grab the bar and have fun. Like Sheriff Tracy said, see for yourself what happens next. Know for yourself how this feels."

I look around me. We're so high up here. I look at the trees around the edge of the open field and gauge that I'm around thirty feet in the air. There are low-hanging clouds around the tops of the trees. There's a breeze swaying through their branches, but I don't hear a sound from them. I see a sweet cottage on the other side of the trees. It's white with green trim and looks like the perfect place to find the perfect glass of lemonade.

Climb down the ladder and get some lemonade, invites the Admin. I look down at the net. *That net doesn't look as big as it did when we were on the ground,* the Admin observes.

As if she can hear the Admin herself, Juliette responds, "Those are just perceptions racing around your mind. Here, dip your hands into the chalk bucket and coat them."

I do as she says. Giuseppe has brought the bar back and now holds it in front of me. I look to him and he smiles. I look to Juliette and she gives me a reassuring nod. She seems so confident that I can do this. They all do. Maybe I can do this.

I look straight at the bar and grip it with my left hand. My right is holding tight to the same vertical pole Sheriff Tracy gripped before. "Excellent," says Juliette. "Now move your feet so your toes are at the edge of the platform. Giuseppe and I have a hold of your waist, so don't worry." My feet and I, still on the same team, move together until the front edge of my toes meets the edge of the platform.

"Perfect," says Juliette. "Take a deep breath in and blow it out." I do as she says. "Take another deep breath in, hold it, then nod and we'll let you go. It's up to you to take the bar in both hands and hop off."

Wait! says the Admin. She sounds panicked.

"This moment is for you, Gail," says Juliette. "This is for you."

I look straight ahead. "For me," I say aloud. The Admin steps back and disappears. I take a deep breath in. I hold it. I nod. They let go of me. My right hand grips the bar hard. I step out.

There are no words. There is wind and force and power. I am moving fast. An idea to close my eyes enters my head, but I push it away. My eyes are open. I'm flying! The force of my body through the air is powerful, frightening, exhilarating, and loud. I swing across the sky and come up, up, up to a point where I could touch the low-hanging clouds above me. They look soft. I see a bird a few feet away who looks over and meets my gaze. Then everything reverses. I'm moving back with the same force, the same power, the same wind in my ears. I hear voices too. They're cheering. The sound of their joyful shouts for me is wonderful. I feel tears well in my eyes.

I hear Sheriff Tracy call to me, "Let go when you hear the *hup!*"

I remember about the *hup*, though my mind makes a choice not to process that I will fall next. There's only one way off this ride. An image of the cottage through the trees appears in my head, and I look for it. I see its white clapboard siding with green trim. The cottage is cheering me too. I'm glad I skipped the lemonade.

I return full swing to where I began and start to move forward for the second time. I look straight ahead and see the pole at the other end. I only see the pole. I focus on it so hard that everything goes quiet, like the world is holding its breath for me. I hear a sharp and clear *hup!*

I let go. I want to scream but I don't. I feel my body fall. I think to move myself back a bit, be a plank. I don't know if it's working, but as I think this thought I get the answer. I reach the net, landing on my butt first and then feeling it envelope the rest of me before shooting me back up into the air again. I don't fly far. I'm back in the net in the next instant. After some more minor bouncing, my body settles into the net. I lie there. I hear cheering and shouting around me. I remain motionless. I did it. I took the ride and now it's over. I start to laugh. I giggle at first but then I let loose and I laugh hard and loud. I laugh and roll to my side, thinking I might try to stand on the net except I'm laughing too hard. I tumble back into the net where I lay flat and just let myself laugh.

Below the net, right below me, Steve and Sheriff Tracy are standing and watching me. After a few moments, Steve asks, "Are you okay? Can you come off the net?" His voice startles me. I stop laughing and look down to see he's looking up at me through the net.

His face is a mix of delight and concern. It strikes me as odd and makes me burst out in another round of laughter. Even so, I roll my way to the edge of the net. With Steve and the sheriff's help, I manage to dismount. After reaching the ground and giving both Sheriff Tracy and Steve a grateful hug, I turn to Steve with pride and boom at him, *"Your turn!"*

CHAPTER 7

*T*wenty minutes ago, I would never have believed that I could do something better than Steve, especially something like flying on a trapeze for the first time. I cheer him on and yell that if I can do it so can he. When he finally starts, he hangs on during the swing but screams his head off the whole time. I see him squeeze his eyes shut three seconds into his ride. Poor guy doesn't hear the *hup* when it's offered by Giuseppe, so Steve has to take an extra pass to get into position for the fall. When he makes it back to center, still yelling – and at a higher pitch even – all four of us yell *hup* in unison, which causes him to let go. He lands fine on his back, though he continues to scream a bit while his body sinks into the net. His screaming tapers off to what sounds like dry heaving. Then that stops after a few moments.

Sheriff Tracy and I help Steve off the net. He looks shaken and relieved that the ride is over. "Well, I did it," Steve says to us. We chuckle, hug, and congratulate him. Sheriff Tracy calls up to Giuseppe and Juliette, who are still on the platform, "That's all we have time for now. Thanks so much!" Giuseppe and Juliette wave to us and blow kisses to Sheriff Tracy, who blows kisses back up at them.

Juliette then takes the bar and gives us the gift of seeing what a seasoned pro can do on a trapeze. We watch as Juliette soars through the air with beauty and confidence. Her art and her talent are inspiring. I open my mouth to say that Juliette looks as though she belongs up there flying through the air like a bird. I close my mouth when I realize that she does belong up in the air. It's not an act. This is her passion and her life. She's made to do this. I want that. I want to spend my time doing what I love. I want to dream again.

I turn to Steve and say to him, "If nothing else happens, then this was worth the trip."

He smiles and says, "I'm glad to hear you say that. I, however, am still waiting for my stomach to find its way off my tailbone and back to my midsection where it belongs. I also look forward to when my ears stop ringing from my own panic-stricken screaming. But you looked great up there. Do you think there's more trapeze flying in your future?"

I shrug. "I don't know, maybe. I could not do that again and be very grateful for the one ride I did take." We turn to Sheriff Tracy, who has put her shirt, pants, and shoes back on. I love knowing what's under her uniform. It makes me wonder what other people have lying in wait just below their outer covering.

"Thank you, Sheriff Tracy," I say to her. "Thank you for doing this for us today."

"It's my pleasure, really," says our sheriff. "Let's get going to Ned's field now." She looks at her watch. "We're going to make it just in time."

"What happens after we get to Portland?" Steve asks Sheriff Tracy. "What do we do next?"

"I don't know. You'll figure that out when you get there, I suppose," says Sheriff Tracy.

We get in her squad car and we take off. My heart says a fond good-bye to the clouds and the birds, the cottage and the trapeze, Giuseppe and Juliette – my new friends. In a few minutes, I'll say good-bye to Sherriff Tracy. My heart aches at the thought. I'm braver today than I've ever been thanks to her.

"How long have you been swinging on a trapeze, Sherriff Tracy?" I ask her.

"About a year. I'd have shown off for you some if we'd had the time." She grins her wide grin again. "Not that I'm much better than what you did get to see, but what I can do is get up on the trapeze into a sitting position while I swing, lean backward so I'm dangling at my knees, reach up ahead of me, and grab another bar swinging toward me. It's taken me six months and a lot of time in the net, but I can do it!" She's beaming with pride. "I'm not what you call a natural, but swinging up high is… well, I suppose you know that feeling now." Her eyes smile at me and I smile back.

"Six months seems like a lot of work," I say.

"Sometimes it felt like work, mostly it was fun. There's something in me that has to keep trying. At the end of the day, I just love it."

Ten minutes later we're pulling into another field. This time, instead of a large barn, we see a simple one-story blue house. It looks cozy with its porch swing hung next to the front door. Ned looks content sitting in the swing. As we drive up, Ned meets us at the car. He opens the driver-side door for Sheriff Tracy.

"Hello again, Ned," says the sheriff. "I hope we haven't made you wait long."

"No," replies Ned.

"Good, I'm glad to hear it. Lucy's ready to go?"

"Yep," says Ned, a bastion of brevity.

"Excellent." Sheriff Tracy turns to Steve and I while Ned makes his way to the back of his house. "Well, I know we're about to part ways, but I'm not quite done with you – just a sec." Sheriff Tracy goes to the trunk of her car and pulls out a briefcase. She closes the trunk door and sets the case on top of it, opens the case, and pulls out a large envelope. "I kept this in the car in case my husband had a miracle recovery, and we could take off at any moment to make the Celebration of Light festival. Now I see I really kept it close so I could give it to you two." Sheriff Tracy hands me the envelope. "In there are two tickets to tonight's show and directions on where to find your viewing area. Vietnam is competing tonight."

I open my mouth to say it's too much and we can't take the tickets, but Sheriff Tracy raises her right hand so it's flat in front of my mouth to stop me. Her left hand reaches into her left shirt pocket and pulls out a business card. "I'm not going to accept a 'no' on this and I'm also not going to accept any money. What you can do is call and tell me how the show goes. You're going to be back for Steve's plane anyway. Call me when you're back in town." She hands me her business card. "I was really looking forward to seeing what Vietnam brings. Just the thought of Vietnam competing is so exciting. Can you imagine those folks making a show and bringing it from somewhere as exotic as Vietnam?! So you are on your honor to enjoy that show for me and report back."

With that, Sheriff Tracy opens her arms wide. I happily walk into a hug with her. I feel tears well up as she gives me a tight squeeze, then I let go so she can give Steve a hug too.

"Thank you for everything, Sheriff Tracy," says Steve as they hug.

"It's my pleasure," she replies. "You two really turned my day around. Those tickets were getting to feel pretty heavy in the trunk of my car. Now go have some fun!"

"Thank you," I say, wishing there was a grander way to express how I feel.

"You're very welcome, Gail."

Steve and I watch her drive away. Neither of us has words for the gifts we've been given by the good sheriff, so we walk silently around Ned's house to find him standing next to Steve's plane.

"Come on." He waves us to follow him around Steve's plane. We obey while we look around, wondering where Ned's plane can be. We find Ned standing on the opposite side of Steve's plane next to what looks like a tin box with wings. We both stop dead. This contraption can't possibly fly. There's no door on the side of the plane, and it's so small that it doesn't look as though it seats more than one person.

"What model of plane is this, Ned?" asks Steve. His voice has a fearful tremor.

"She's a Boeing L-15 Scout," Ned tells us. He steps to the back of the plane and opens two vertical door panels that are functionally the back wall of the plane when they're closed. The doors are clear plastic, like large windows. Out of instinct, I reach over and grab Steve's arm. Steve takes my hand and brings it through his arm while keeping hold of it. He starts us walking toward the plane together. We reach the back of the plane, where Ned still stands, and we look into it. The entire inside of the plane is a space that is maybe four feet wide and ten feet long. There are two chairs inside, one chair for the pilot at the front and a bucket seat at the back that swivels. I see there are seat belts in the chairs, which makes me bark out a single laugh. Scared that I've offended Ned, my free hand flies to my mouth as I look over to him.

Ned responds with an amused grin. "I'd be surprised if you didn't laugh. She's a small girl but she's got a lot of spunk." With that, Ned gets in the plane and sits in the pilot's seat. Over his shoulder, he calls out to us, "Gail should get in and sit in the middle on the floor. I need Steve in the back seat for balance."

Steve gives my hand a squeeze and lets it go. This is his prompt for me to get in. There is barely any space on either side of the back chair so I sit in it and swivel myself around. There is just enough room between the two chairs for me to sit. I put my back against one wall and plant my feet against the wall opposite. I'm not a tall person. That my legs can stretch the width of the plane puts spikes of fear down my spine. As soon as I'm seated, Steve swivels the rear seat back and sits in it. Ned instructs Steve on how to latch the back doors and tells him to fasten his seatbelt, which makes me bark out another involuntary laugh.

Once again, Ned gives me an amused side glance over his shoulder and then goes about the business of starting the plane engine and taxiing us down his back lawn. I hug my knees tight as we take off, expecting this small craft to have to skip twice before leaving Earth. Lucy does no such skipping, however, and gracefully pulls herself into the air. Steve reaches down with one hand and rubs circles on my back to say I can loosen my grip and sit up. We're in the air and flying with no drama at all.

Three minutes into the flight, Ned turns himself a few inches in his chair to speak to me. He has to shout over the noise in this confined space. Seems Lucy's design didn't include any sound-dampening materials in her walls. "Gail, shift yourself up on your knees so you see out the windows." I look up at Steve, who holds his hand out to steady me, while I raise myself like a defiant sardine wanting to stand out in the can. I look out the large windows of Lucy and see that we're maybe fifty feet above a tall tree line.

"The sky looks enormous," shouts Steve. "I know that sounds obvious, but I can't remember the sky looking this wide and big to me before."

"Yep," confirms Ned.

Yep, I think to myself. It's beautiful. The sky is indeed big. The trees are green and beautiful and so close to the plane that I can see twigs at the ends of the top branches. I can also see bird nests in the tops of some trees. In one, I see a large bird like a hawk that looks up at us with an angry stare as we pass by. I can't say I blame her. I'd be mad if a plane buzzed my bed, just missing it by a few feet. I decide to sit back down. No longer feeling defiant, the sardine gets herself back into position on the floor of the tin can. Though I don't feel safe and snug on the floor – more like squished – it's better than teetering on my knees and having to witness how close to nature Ned keeps this fragile, thin-walled box with wings.

I call up to Ned. "How long until we get to Portland?"

"Thirty minutes," Ned tells me.

Great, I think, thirty more squished minutes to go.

And then what? asks the Admin. I feel her planting herself on my chest, which I'm sure she enjoys, although, to be fair, there's nowhere else for her to sit.

I'm not sure, I tell her. *There's no room in this plane for you. Go away.*

Please, Gail, where you go, I go. Right now, you want me here, she boasts. *You're ready to talk sense.*

Am I? I refuse to be on her side, even though I feel it in this moment. *I just proved myself to be a budding trapeze artist. Why shouldn't I be soaring through the air in a museum relic of a plane?*

You've done enough today, states the Admin. *The trapeze was enough to* last you a year. If you go to that festival, then you're not getting home in time for the kids. You know that.

I know.

You haven't called John to tell him what you're doing, reminds the Admin. He's going to worry about you and he doesn't deserve that.

No, he doesn't.

You are going to call John when we land, she orders, with an impatient clip.

I don't know if I can, is my sheepish counter.

How can you not call your husband to tell him where you are? The Admin is mad at me now. I can understand the anger.

I don't think I'm ready to explain any of this to him. I'm not sure how to explain it to myself yet.

You're just being a coward, same as usual, says the Admin, or I wouldn't be here.

Excuse me?

Your elation for achieving flight made you blind and deaf to what matters, the Admin continues.

What matters?

Stop being stupid, moron. Your family is what matters – your responsibilities to them and to your work. You created your life. Now you're responsible for it. There's a lot of work to do to take care of what you created. You don't just turn your back on all that to go joy riding with the first handsome stranger who pays attention to you. The Admin is right. How exactly are you getting home today? And when you get home, what exactly are you going to say?

I don't know yet. I'll figure it out on my way home. First, I have to figure out a way home, I acquiesce.

Good – the Admin is glad I'm submissive again – one issue at a time. Let's concentrate on the first one. How can we get you home today? We both think on this question. I could rent a car or buy a plane ticket. A wave of sadness falls on me when I picture myself at an airline ticket counter. I don't want to go home. I'm not ready. I'm not done with today. I'm a bad person.

You have a life others wish they had. This is one of the Admin's favorite tunes. *Your husband is a good man. More than that, he's your man. He describes himself as being hard-coded for you. Your kids are beautiful and healthy and smart. You have a job that pays you a lot of money and gives you benefits that impress your doctors when you see them.*

That's the part that's hard. That last one, I say.

Having a high-paying job with stellar benefits? Getting to work with a team of extraordinary people is hard for you? The Admin is shrill with disgust. My throat feels constricted. I try to swallow, but my throat feels blocked. My job keeps me and my family safe. I'm grateful for it. I'm grateful I have my job and I grieve about it. Each day I'm faced with not wanting to do again what I do every day – a whole lot of nothing I enjoy. It chips away at me.

Who are you to want more? the Admin asks with a sneer. *It's ridiculous that you're sitting in this plane. You have everything in life that matters. Yet, when the opportunity presented itself, you ran away. No, you didn't just run. You got in a plane to leave the country with a stranger. This is all your fault for wishing for something different to happen today.*

Yes. You're right. I did wish for something different. I want something in my life that doesn't feel like work.

You, you, you, goads the Admin.

Yes, me. The defiant sardine is back. *I'm not going to make it home in time for the kids. I'm not going to tuck them into bed tonight. I'll have to explain to John that I left the country for the day, and why. Maybe all of that is okay.*

John won't get them to bed on time, the Admin reminds me. *He doesn't watch the clock like you do. He doesn't watch the clock at all.*

True, but he doesn't have to when I'm there, does he? He's a good dad. He'll get them to bed, eventually, I counter the Admin.

He won't get them up on time in the morning. He can't get himself out of bed on time. He doesn't know how to make their lunches...

He'll figure it out! Geez, give the man a break. He's a smart guy. Besides, I'll be back by morning. I have work tomorrow. I say this to impress on the Admin that I've remembered my job. *I'll call him when we land and work it out. They'll survive one night without me. I'm not ready to go home yet. Go away.* The Admin gets up and walks to the back of my head. She sits there fuming, though satisfied. She made her points. Even when I banish her to the back of my head, I am ever aware of the Admin and her disgust with me.

I wiggle my way back up to my knees. Steve helps me.

"Did you want another look before we land?" Steve asks.

"Yes and no. The view is great, but the small size and antique look of this plane is kind of freaking me out." I try to say this without Ned hearing. I have no idea if I succeeded.

"I know what you mean," says Steve. "I think Lucy was built around World War II. Ned seems to know what he's doing, though."

"Do we know what we're doing?" I ask Steve.

"The plan is to go to the Celebration of Lights festival tonight and see a rocking fireworks show straight from Vietnam." Steve is emphatic.

"What about Aria?" I ask him.

"I'll call some friends who have a kid in the same class as her. They can sign her out and take her home for the night. I've done the same for their son when they were in a bind."

Great, Steve has it covered. He's not worried about not getting back.

"I guess it's time to call John and tell him where you are, huh?" Though he has to shout this question at me to be heard, there is distinct kindness and understanding in his asking.

"I guess so," I reply.

Ned bends his head around to speak to us. "We're about to land. Take a seat, Gail."

CHAPTER 8

*N*ed pilots Lucy to the ground with ease. He makes it look easy. As deft as he is as a pilot, I find that having us stopped on the ground allows me to breathe again. Ned shuts down the engines and instructs Steve to open the doors and get out. I maneuver myself off the floor and into the back seat. I swivel hard in a rush to leave and almost find myself facing Ned again. Leaving Lucy is a big relief. Though she's a wonder, Lucy is a loud and rickety old girl that I'd be happy never to enter again.

"Where are we?" I ask Ned.

"You're on a US Postal Service airstrip. The Portland airport is next to us." Ned nods his head in the direction of a larger terminal building about half a mile away.

"We're making our way to Vancouver," Steve tells him.

"Know how you're getting there?" Ned asks.

"Not really, no." Steve looks around. "I guess we could buy a ticket at the airport."

"I may be able to help," says Ned. "This airstrip is international with Canada mail."

"Any help would be appreciated," says Steve. "It may save us time to hitch another ride."

"Uh-huh," Ned agrees.

"We also need to coordinate how to get back to you so I can get my plane," says Steve.

"Yep," says Ned, and he hands Steve a card that he takes from his wallet.

Steve looks at the card and starts a bit when he reads it. "Your name is Ned Boeing."

"Yep," Ned confirms.

"Are you part of the Boeing family that makes Boeing airplanes, Ned?" asks Steve.

"I'm a relation of that family, yessir."

"Sheriff Tracy said you worked as a mechanic for Boeing," I say to him.

"I did," says Ned.

"If you don't mind me asking," says Steve, "were the executive offices not to your liking?"

"I don't mind you asking," says Ned. "I don't belong up there, never did." Ned notices the expectant looks on our faces as we wait for further explanation. "So I left it to be a mechanic."

"That seems like a lot to walk away from," says Steve. He sounds impressed with Ned. I can't imagine walking away from anything that secure. His name is on the letterhead, for Pete's sake.

"I got Lucy out of the deal," Ned tells us, "after I helped to restore her. They bring me in at air shows to fly her around. That's enough for me."

We stand there waiting for the next words out of Ned's mouth. It seems as though Ned is waiting too. I look to Steve, who seems transfixed by Ned. I wish I could understand whatever it is that impresses him about Ned. What's so great about giving up a piece of a large and lucrative pie?

"Well," Ned says. I think it is the beginning of something more, but he turns and walks away. Steve and I watch him for a minute, then we both sigh at the same time. I can't imagine we're sighing for the same reasons, however.

"What do you see in him?" I ask Steve.

"Hope."

"Hope for what?"

Steve thinks my question through for a moment. I like that he doesn't have all the answers at the tip of his tongue. "Hope that I might be brave enough one day to stop chasing after money and just live," says Steve. "If Ned can do it, then I think I could do it too." Darn it. That's a nice answer.

A few more moments pass as we wait for Ned's return. Steve turns to me and looks into my eyes for something. He doesn't look as though he's finding what he hoped to find. I open my mouth to ask what his deal is, but he beats me to the first words. "You were going to call John now to tell him about today."

A ripple of anxiety courses up from my feet. It travels straight up me like a ribbon that exits through the top of my head and stops. The top tail of the ribbon floats above my head, waiting for some invisible giant to tug at my anxiety and force me to dance in it. On cue, my giant appears.

You forgot about John – again, admonishes the Admin. *Time to face the music, Gail. Call John.*

I look down at my purse. I see that my anxiety has me strangling the strap. I look up at Steve and nod to let him know I'll be making that call now. He nods back and walks toward Lucy. I watch Steve take his own phone out to make his call home for Aria. There's no hesitation or fear in his action.

Make the call, orders the Admin. *Stop stalling.*

I look down at my purse again, and I try to act like Steve. I take a breath, open my purse, find my phone, and dial. I hear the phone engage and start ringing. Each ring tugs at the ribbon of my anxiety. I'm fixated on the rings, waiting for them to stop and to hear John's voice – or maybe I'll get the voice mail. I'd be relieved to get the voice mail, but what would I say? What am I about to say to him now if he answers? I could ask how he's doing, so he starts talking first.

"Hey there, rebel," says John, who has answered the phone in the middle of my mounting panic attack. What did he say?

"What?"

"I just said hi to the new family rebel. Playing hooky from work is not something I've ever seen you do, but here you are," cheers John. "You lied to your boss even." I think he's kidding with me, but he's hitting nerves. "Who are you and what have you done with Gail?" I don't know what to say. "Gail? Are you still there?"

"Uhhhhhhh, I'm here."

"What fun thing are you up to? Did you need something?"

Right now doesn't feel like fun.

Tell him, instructs the Admin.

I'm paralyzed. I want to tell him everything. I don't want to tell him anything. He's my best friend and cheerleader. He'll understand. He's going to be hurt that I went on an adventure without him. I'm not alone. I'm with another man and not him. I would be hurt if the tables were turned. I would be jealous and hurt and angry.

"Gail, are you okay? Is something wrong?" Great, now I'm scaring him. Yes, John, something is wrong. I'm wrong.

"I'm okay," I say.

"Good," I can hear his relief. He loves me, and he needs me. I don't want to hurt him.

"I'm fine. I called because I'm going to be home late. I won't be home in time to pick up the kids." I listen to my voice for clues he might hear. Can he hear in the words I'm speaking that I'm standing on an airstrip in Portland, Oregon?

"Oh, that's fine. I can get the kids," says John. "When do you think you'll be home?"

"I think I'm going to be late. You shouldn't wait up for me." I hold my breath after speaking these last words.

"Weeelll, what are you up to, huh? Going to a strip club? Hitting a few bars? Feel free to wake me when you get home."

"Ha, ha," I say. I'm about to correct him about the strip club but remember that I should hold my tongue. I'll tell him later what I did today. I'll tell him when I get home. It'll be better to tell him when I'm in the same room as him. "I'm not sure what's going to happen next or when exactly I'll be home. I just wanted to call so you know to get the kids, and so you don't worry."

"Sure, sweetie, thanks for the call," John says. "I'm glad you're taking a break. I love you."

"I love you." My heart tugs as I say this. I'm lying to him, and it feels like the right thing to do.

The Admin is quick to contradict me. *You're wrong to do this to him. You're a heartless failure.*

"I have to let you go. I'll see you when you get home or in the morning. I can't wait to hear what you did today. Make it good!" says my husband.

"Thanks, honey," I reply, and with that John hangs up. I look down at my phone and watch as the screen notifies me that the call has ended. Talking to John went better than I thought it would. I'm off the hook. I'm relieved. Is that bad?

Yes! You failed. You lied. You're a failure. You're wrong, chants the Admin.

"How'd it go?" asks Steve as he walks back to me.

I think about what to say to Steve. I can't look him in the eye. The chants of the Admin are ringing in my head. "I think it went okay."

"He wasn't mad?" asks Steve.

"No," I say. "I told him I'd be home late and that he shouldn't wait up for me."

"Did you tell him anything else?"

"No, not really," I say. "I told him I wasn't sure what was going to happen next or when I'd be home. He says he can't wait to hear about what I do and that I should make it good."

"You look hurt," observes Steve.

"I feel like shit saying this out loud to you."

Steve can see in my face the shame that is piling itself on top of the hurt. "Let's think this through," he says. "Do you want to call John back?"

"No," I say with instant guilt. "I don't know. What do you think I should do?"

"I think you should go to the Celebration of Light Festival with me in Vancouver tonight," says Steve. "I think you should do what's best for you. John sounds like a solid guy, so he'll understand when you tell him later. If he doesn't understand, then it doesn't mean it was wrong of you to be on this trip with me. If he can't see the good this is doing you, then something else is wrong." Steve sees my shoulders slump even lower. "Gail, I'm not sure what to say."

"It would hurt you to hear your wife went off on a day like today without you," I state.

"Yeah, that would sting. I'd like to think I'd get over it, though." Steve smiles at me and I feel warm.

"I'm glad you're here with me and not at home."

I'm not sure I'm happy about this moment, but it seems to work – John knows I'm okay and that I'll be home late. It's not the whole truth, but it feels like it's enough, at least for now. I put my phone back in my purse. The Admin opens her mouth to rail on me, but I put a hand in front of her face that shuts her down for now. I know silencing her means greater grief from her later, but I've reached my limit for the time being.

Steve gives my shoulder a nudge and smiles a comic grin to get me to smile too. I attempt a smile but it falters. Then something unexpected and wonderful happens. Steve hugs me. It isn't a quick hug either. He holds me. Being held by him and against him has both a warmth and a heat that I want to bathe in. I don't want it to end. He seems content to let me linger there, so I do. I take a long breath in through my nose to saturate myself in his smell. There's no cologne that I can make out, just the leather of his jacket mixed with the right amount of man musk that's enticing instead of odorous.

Right before the Admin is about to sucker punch me, I peel myself away from Steve. I take my time.

"Thanks," I tell him while my eyes dart around for something to fixate on besides him. I look around at the Portland postal airstrip. There are several small planes surrounding us. Lucy is by far the most interesting. I'm stunned to think that just a few minutes ago I was flying through the air in her. Farther away down the airfield are larger planes with the US Postal Service insignia on them. In the far distance, I see the forests we flew over. I wonder if the hawk that we disturbed has forgiven us yet. Do hawks remember things like that? Or are we out of her mind already?

"I'm hungry," announces Steve. "It's lunchtime. Maybe we should find some food."

I check in with my stomach. My stomach tells me I'm hungry too. "Lunch is a great idea. Maybe there's something in the Post Office hangar or the larger airport terminal."

"Let's find Ned and see if he has any travel leads for us. Then we can get some food," suggests Steve.

We walk in the same direction Ned went when he left us, toward a one-story building at the edge of the airfield. My stomach has my attention now. The hunger pains are starting to grow, so I try to think of something else. I'm glad I got to skip my commute today. The hour it takes to get to work, and the hour-ish it takes to get home are soul-leaching times. There's only so much public radio with DJs trying to make the mundane laughable that I can handle. Silence is worse. Silence is when the Admin creeps up on me to rehash how I'm letting down two or more people at any given time, most often myself. Lunchtime is my favorite part of the working day. If I were at work, I'd be gathering with the coworkers I consider friends to walk together to the campus cafeteria. We're all full of stories for each other. They tell me stories about parties on the weekends, and I relay funny anecdotes about my kids. They each have hobbies that are fascinating. One finds and restores vintage clothing that she turns around and sells online. Another has an extreme love of Volvos and owns at least five at a time that he's rebuilding, driving around himself, or selling. The second bedroom in his apartment is a Volvo salvage yard. I've seen it. There's no way he's getting his cleaning deposit back.

I realize my friends at work may be wondering what the emergency is that kept me from work today. I'm going to have some great stories for tomorrow's lunchtime. I may be the grand champion of stories told at lunch for some time to come. My stories will fade after a while, though. Other stories will be told. I want today to stick with me. I can feel. I'm not just analyzing and tracking what I have to do today. I'm feeling. The thought of going back to my regular routine makes my empty stomach turn. Lunchtimes are such a small part of the work day. I need something more in my life to feed me – something for me.

Adding something else to my day is nigh impossible, though. My boys take up my hobby time. It doesn't seem right to spend less time with my kids. I get a couple of hours in the morning and a couple of hours at night with them during the work week, and then the weekends. The weekends are taken up with frantic efforts to try and regain ground in our messy, cluttered house. If there was a pie chart made of what I do with my time, then a big chunk would go to my job, a sizable chunk would go to my house, and an impressive piece would go to the time spent lecturing my boys about picking up after themselves or taking turns with a toy without wrestling for it. The pie chart doesn't show time left for me.

The pie chart also doesn't tell me how to be okay with the cluttered house while I do some sewing instead. It doesn't tell me how to get my husband and sons to see the clutter and help me out without needing instructions from me that they've heard a million times before. Oprah has tried to help me, and I love her for it. Still, even with all her advice, I can't seem to climb over the mountainous to-do list. Oprah tells me I have to change if my life is going to change and I believe her, and the amount of work it takes to run my life doesn't lessen. I want to figure this out or all anyone is going to say about me at my funeral is how dependable I was. I've grown to hate being dependable. I want to be magical, and creative, and in love with myself, and live in a clean house. I have no idea how that happens.

ACT 2

The Other Hero

CHAPTER 9

*J*ohn's call with Gail is short but sweet. It makes him happy when she calls to check in with him, which she does without fail. What thrills John is that Gail is taking the day off. Though it surprises him that his straitlaced, overachieving wife is taking a day for herself, he hopes it will become a trend.

John puts his phone down and turns back to his computer to continue the code work on his latest project. He could not be happier with the contract he has now designing for Virgin Galactic, the private space shuttle program owned by Richard Branson. Sir Richard has decreed that his space shuttle program, which promises rides into space for those who can afford them, needs an android flight attendant. John has been hired to design and program the hands that will serve the vacuum-sealed bags of champagne to the passengers of the Virgin Galactic spacecraft. Seriously, it doesn't get much better than this.

John is in the middle of a sticky piece of code that gets the android hand to grab the bag firmly enough so it doesn't float away, but doesn't over-grip and burst the bag of Moët champagne – oh yes, Branson packs the good champagne on his shuttle. John starts a process running and then turns to look at his robot arm, which is covered in plastic sheeting and affixed to a table five feet away from anything expensive. On a stool next to the table sits a juice pouch John stole from the kitchen. Working from home has its perks.

The intricate hand at the end of the robot arm pokes out from the plastic. The fingers start to flex open as the arm extends them toward the juice pouch. The arm positions the hand perfectly so the fingers and thumb are on either side of the pouch. The fingers contract slowly. They stop just as the pouch is showing signs of bulging from the pressure. The arm lifts the hand and extends outward as though offering the pouch to an invisible person. John jumps up from his chair and assumes the role of space shuttle passenger. He gently tugs at the top of the pouch, signaling to the hand that it can release the drink. The fingers of the hand start to open a fraction and then they contract abruptly, causing the juice to explode all over John.

John's face is coated in fruit punch. That includes his eyelids, which are squeezed shut, signaling to him that he forgot the first rule of science experimentation: wear safety goggles. John allows his left eye to open just enough to look over at his workbench and see his goggles sitting there looking back at him. Fruit punch drops fall from his eyebrows onto his eyelashes, causing his eye to slam shut again. John gropes for the utility sink and washes the juice from his face, neck, arms, and chest, and gets most of it out of his hair. He looks down at himself and makes a new rule of science: have a spare change of clothing in a large sealable plastic bag stored in the workbench. He knows Gail would kill him if he dripped fruit punch up the stairs and down the hall to their bedroom. He must strip to get more clothes from upstairs. Another perk of working at home: sudden bursts of nudity in the workplace are allowed. John figures, as he removes his shirt and pants, that a shower can wait until after his next round of tries with the arm and more juice pouches.

Shower... the hint of a memory enters John's head. Gail told him something about the shower last night. What did she say? She asked him to do something. John strains to remember, but it's not there. Gail even made sure he was paying attention to her. She made John stop his work and look at her so his attention wasn't split. However,

John's mind was still at his workbench even though he was looking straight at her.

"Damn," John thinks aloud. "She's going be ticked if she comes home, and I didn't do whatever she asked me to do." John tries hard to remember, but he cannot recall her words. "I was in the shower this morning. I didn't see anything wrong with it. Maybe she wants me to buy soap or shampoo. We have soap. That it isn't it." A large weight starts to press on John's chest. He hates disappointing Gail. She'll probably be okay with him forgetting, but it's a political boost when he remembers something she asked of him.

John resolves that he has to call Gail. He knows that showing her he has a partial memory that she said something is better than a total failure to do anything. John checks his hands to be sure all the sticky juice is washed off before he reaches for his phone on the workbench. He starts to press the speed dial for her phone, then stops. She's having a special day for herself. He doesn't want to interrupt something good for her with his memory fail. Maybe he should text her, John thinks. He opens a text message and then stops again. A text is still an interruption with bad news that he failed to remember something. John thinks to check on where she is using the locator service they have on their phones. He'll be able to tell by her location if she's at a movie or in a favorite restaurant. He can even tell by the locator dot that appears on a map if she's in transit. It'll be better to catch her if she's moving, John thinks. Then she'll follow up his conversation with something fun. Of course, John also knows that if he doesn't try to catch her now, he'll just forget all about this in five minutes.

John selects Gail's name in the locator screen and waits for the dot to appear. The blue dot comes up in a map. Gail's dot looks like it's in an open field. John looks for the closest street next to the field. The street name is NE 47th Avenue. The street name isn't familiar. John zooms out so he gets a better idea of where Gail is standing. His curiosity is piqued. John loves to solve problems. The quicker he finds an answer, the more he gets to brag. John sets himself the challenge of determining where she is by as few hints as possible – the mystery is afoot. John zooms out enough to see that she's in a small field next to large buildings and strips of land. He blinks a couple of times and realizes that it looks like an airport. Wow, is she getting flying lessons?

John looks around the map and sees there is water next to the airport. "She's at the San Francisco airport. Whatever she's doing must be good," he says. He scans the map some more to find a street name he recognizes when he sees the landmark title above a central mass of buildings he figures are the terminals at the airport. John expects his deductions to be proved correct, that she's at the San Francisco airport, but instead the title reads "Portland International Airport." John repeats aloud what his mind just registered to see if it will help him understand what he's seeing. "Portland International Airport." The only Portland he knows is in Oregon. John zooms the map out again until it's reduced to the landscape of a state. The title on the state says Oregon.

This can't be right, John thinks. She can't be in Oregon. This locator thing isn't working. John looks up at his robot arm and sees juice dripping off the fingers of the hand. He puts his phone down and picks up some shop towels so he can clean off the hand and soak up most of the juice on the plastic sheeting. As he works, his mind is still turning over and around the words *Portland International Airport*. The locator service has never fritzed out like this before. Maybe someone stole her phone, thinks John, except she just called him from her phone. I could call her, he thinks. I can ask her about the shower and then casually ask her where she is. She would have told me if she were leaving for Portland. Gail wouldn't leave the state and not tell me. Not my Gail. She's been stressed for sure, but she wouldn't run away. John tries to focus on cleaning the robot hand. The hand mechanisms are covered, so leaving the outer shell of the hand somewhat sticky for the next experiment would have been fine, but John proceeds to do a very thorough job of swabbing up the juice while his mind ruminates on Gail, wondering what she's doing. This work does wonders for the robot, but nothing for John.

John looks over at his phone, uncertain what he should do next. He walks over and picks up his phone and runs the locator service again. Gail is outside one of the buildings next to the smaller field, a field inside the Portland International Airport.

"I just need to call her," John says out loud to see how it sounds. If she's in Portland, then it's for a good reason, a fun reason, he surmises. Except, she would have told him she was going if it were a fun reason. His heart sinks with this thought. His fingers hover over her name in the speed-dial list of his phone. After a staggered couple of breaths, John presses her name and lifts the phone to his ear. He listens to the ringing. Five rings that seem louder and longer as each pass by and then lead to her voice mail. She didn't pick up. Did she hear her phone? John listens to Gail's voice instructing him to leave a message. He hears the tone that the recording has started. For a moment, he doesn't speak. What should he say? Then John remembers the shower.

"Hey, sweetie, sorry to bother you on your day away, but I just remembered you want me to do something with the shower, only I can't remember what you want me to do. Can you call me or text me please?" John pauses, wondering if he should say anything more. He can't get himself to ask about Portland, so he hangs up instead. In the next instant, he regrets not asking about Portland. Now what? Call back? No, John thinks, I'll wait. John puts the phone down on his workbench. His bare chest catches his attention. He realizes he's standing in his workshop in nothing but his underwear. John was in the middle of stripping to get new clothes when this whole tangent with Gail started.

Frustrated, he starts for the stairs to go get some fresh clothes when his text alert goes off. John strides back to his phone and reads the text from Gail: "I asked you to unclog the shower drain please. Thanks for doing this. Can't wait to see you. xxoo"

John turns her text over in his head. Gail says she can't wait to see me. It doesn't sound like she's running, except she's in Oregon. Oregon counts as a run: a run away from home, and a run away from him. A boulder of fear presses down on John. The weight of it is painful. The comfortable and confident blanket of Gail's love slips from his heart. John wants to get the blanket back in place again.

"What do I do?" he asks himself. "I want to find her. I'll go crazy here waiting for her to come back. I don't want to unclog the drain for her if she's not coming back. I can't work on the robot now. I'll do something stupid and break it." John's frustration is punctuated by him reaching up with both hands and grabbing fists of hair. His fingers weave themselves into a pool of sticky juice goo that has matted the hair just above his forehead. This is too much. His mind is about to snap. John takes a breath and decides to get cleaned up. He'll take a shower, and then he'll figure out what comes next. At least, he hopes his brain will kick in and start functioning again so he can think everything through.

John sprints upstairs and gets straight into the shower. While he washes the juice out of his hair, his mind fixates on Gail's dot in the locator service and the words in Gail's text. Two minutes into the shower, John feels a puddle forming around his toes. He looks down to see that water is backing up from the drain and circling his feet. By the time he's done washing out his hair, the water is almost up to his ankles. How did he miss this happening during his shower this morning? His mind was on the robot. He finishes in the shower and turns the water off. He contemplates the drain and thinks of Gail. Ankle deep in a pool of soapy run-off shower water that is saturated with the fruit punch he just washed off himself, John chooses to unclog the drain. He opens the shower door and reaches for a towel that he uses to dry his feet as he steps out of the lake and onto the bath mat. John's anxiety abates somewhat, giving way to quiet determination. He dresses and gets the tools he needs to unclog the drain. All the while sorting through what he's going to do with the knowledge that his wife has gone to Oregon without him.

CHAPTER 10

*I*t doesn't take us long to find Ned in the small building off the airstrip where we just landed. He's speaking with someone dressed in a pilot's uniform. It strikes me as odd that Ned doesn't wear a uniform if this man does. Mr. Boeing is at his job now. He's at the office. Why does he get to be so casual? Ned sees us wandering toward him and waves us over to meet his friend.

"Steve, Gail, this is Frank." We shake Frank's hand as Ned makes this introduction. "Frank flies the afternoon mail run from here into Vancouver."

"That's great," says Steve.

"Unfortunately, Frank isn't allowed to take civilians in the plane with him when he's crossing the border," says Ned.

Uh-oh, crosses my mind.

"Ah, well, that's not so great, but understandable," says Steve, whose good mood bubble from a moment ago has popped. Something in me has popped too. A mini explosion around the area of my diaphragm. A significant detail has just come to the forefront of my mind that should have surfaced from the start. When I say significant, I mean a showstopper.

I don't have my passport.

"Sorry, folks," says Frank, "but I can't help you today. It's just against the rules."

"No worries, Frank, thanks anyway," says Steve as he shakes Frank's hand again.

"Well, good luck to you," says Frank as he extends his hand toward me. I shake it and manage a thank you smile to show Frank there are no hard feelings. My feelings and my diaphragm are stiffening, however. My empty stomach doesn't help. Frank claps Ned on the shoulder and bids him good-bye before walking away.

"Sorry," says Ned.

"Don't worry about it, Ned," says Steve. "We'll figure things out. Hey, do you know of a place to eat around here?"

My phone starts to ring in my purse.

"I do," says Ned.

I reach for my phone to see who's calling me.

"The best place to eat is Nellie's Sandwich Shack in Terminal 1. The egg salad sandwich is the best." Ned is beaming about this sandwich. I make a mental note to order it.

John is calling me. I don't want to take this call. I don't want to lie, or withhold the truth, again.

"Thanks, Ned." Steve extends his hand out to Ned. "Thanks to you and to Lucy for getting us this far. I'll be in touch tomorrow about my plane."

"Yep," says Ned.

My phone stops ringing and goes to voice mail. John is leaving me a message. I know he is. I want to listen to it, or I can ignore it and pretend my phone was off when he called. I look up to see Steve and Ned looking at me. I look back and forth between them, wondering if they see my guilt at not answering my phone, then I clue in that we're saying good-bye to Ned and they must be waiting on me. I offer my hand to Ned, which he takes in one hand then covers with the other. The warmth of both his hands on mine is surprising.

"Gail, I got a few words for you, if you don't mind," says Ned.

I shake my head no.

"You remind me a lot of me," says Ned, "when I worked somewhere I didn't belong." Ned takes a deep breath in and looks at me with kind, yet very keen, eyes. "It's how you see things when you look around you. I can tell you're looking through a dark filter." Ned's words catch me off-guard. "I know how that filter makes the world look. Your sight improved since your time spent with Sheriff Tracy," Ned continues. "Keep doing what's good for you." Ned gives my hand a gentle squeeze before releasing it.

I'm stunned, unable to say anything. He gives me a kind smile, then walks back into the small building. I look to Steve, who has a strange expression on his face. "Please tell me what you're thinking," I say to him.

"I think Ned may have reached his quota of words he'll speak in a year just then, and I could see that John called," Steve states.

My whole body seems to jump at these words. I look down at my phone that is still in my hand.

"Did he leave a message?" Steve asks.

I navigate to my voice mail and see that there is, in fact, a message from John. I look up at Steve, who still has the strange expression on his face, though now I think I understand it. He looks expectant, like he's waiting on me for something. I look down at my phone again and press John's name in the mail queue so I can hear his message. I look over at Steve as I lift the phone to my ear. His face now looks relieved. I'm about to ask him why he looks so relieved when I hear John's voice in my ear.

"Hey, sweetie, sorry to bother you on your day away, but I just remembered you want me to do something with the shower…"

His voice sounds strained, probably something to do with his robot arm or forgetting the shower. I think for a moment on what to do: call or text. It doesn't take me long to decide that I'm going to text. I'll give John the whole story about today when I'm home, which is likely sooner than I hoped it would be. I enter the most honest words I can into my message to him and press send.

I wait a few seconds to see if he texts me back, or calls. I'm scared. The Admin is looking over my shoulder at the phone as well. She doesn't speak, but her close proximity makes my whole body rigid. Nothing happens with the phone. I don't seem able to move.

"Gail?" asks Steve. "Are you okay?" Hearing Steve breaks me from my trance.

"I don't feel okay," I confess.

"Let's eat," suggests Steve. He takes a small step and then another toward the main terminal, all the while looking over his shoulder at me to be sure I follow. My left foot takes a step and then my right foot. My feet put me in motion. Without looking at my phone, too scared I'll freeze up again, I put it away in my purse. The Admin is in lockstep behind me. I feel her stare boring a hole right through me. We all walk in silence together, for now.

We reach the main terminal and start to wander inside, looking for food. We turn a corner and I see the lines for security. People shuffle forward, removing their shoes and taking laptops out of bags. I see parents with small kids. A mom looks frazzled as she keeps an eye on one child playing with the cord divider that keeps them in their lane, while another child is sitting on her right foot, holding on to her with his arms and legs. I know how she feels as she lifts him to shuffle forward. I know how tired her body is from the packing and from managing the details that got them this far. Lifting the kid on her foot is tough, but at least she has him corralled. I miss my kids.

"Hey, we found Nellie's," Steve says. I look in the direction he's pointing and see an open restaurant that has a '50s diner look. The red vinyl booths remind me of my favorite show as a kid, *Happy Days*. I wonder if Nellie will come out and banter with us in her short order cook uniform like Arnold did on the show. Steve and I walk past a sign that instructs us to please seat ourselves. We find a booth along the back wall and scooch into opposite benches. Menus are on the table. We each take a look, but put them down after a minute. We both know what we want.

A waitress comes over to take our order. Her name tag says she's Alice, another reminder of a TV character I loved as a child. If Mr. Kotter and Mr. Roarke show up, then I'll know this day has been a dream all along. "Hi, what can I get you?" Alice asks us.

"I'll have an egg salad sandwich on wheat bread, please, and a lemonade," I tell her.

"I'll also have an egg salad sandwich on wheat, but I'd like a chocolate milkshake – as thick as you can make it, please," says Steve.

"Will do – I'll be back with some water for you."

Steve and I look at each other. We don't say anything, though it feels like there's so much to say. He has the expectant look on his face again.

"How are you doing?" I ask.

"I think I'm doing okay," he affirms. "I'll be better after some food. Getting a ride in Lucy was a trip, an honor, really, since she looked like a rare old bird."

"She belongs in a museum," I declare with confidence.

"Maybe, but if she can fly, then I think she belongs in the air still."

I shrug my shoulders.

"It didn't look like a very comfortable ride for you, though," says Steve. I shake my head no. My head feels very heavy to me. I look around for Alice and our water. I watch her return with two glasses.

"I'll be back with the milkshake and lemonade," Alice tells us.

I sip at the water and then start to gulp it. Today seems to have made me dehydrated. I drain the glass and then look around for Alice to get more. Steve offers me his glass, which I down gratefully.

"I'll flag Alice for more water if she looks over here," says Steve. "Maybe we should pick up some water bottles while we're here in the airport."

We're in an airport, I think.

That's right, agrees the Admin.

I can just go home.

Yes, confirms the Admin.

I should. I should find the next flight to San Francisco and be on it.

Good. The Admin is pleased. *The ride back will be restful. You deserve a rest.*

I do. I'm tired. I just want to lie down in my bed and sleep for a week.

I know, but there's work and kids tomorrow. You can sleep in one of the mornings this weekend. The Admin has scheduled in my rest break. She keeps a strict calendar.

That's days away, I complain.

"Here you go." Alice puts lemonade in front of me and gives Steve his milkshake. There's a straw in the milkshake that Steve tries to use, but the shake is too thick to bring any liquid up through the narrow passage of the straw.

"Nice," Steve praises. "They know what they're doing here. This is a thick milkshake." Steve picks up his spoon and starts to eat the shake. He looks over at me. "Do you want some?"

"No," I answer. "There have to be six hundred calories in just that spoonful."

"Come on," Steve says as he pushes the milkshake toward me. "I'm sure there's just fifty calories a spoonful – live a little."

"No thanks." I stand firm, sipping my lemonade, which I know has calories too, but it can't be as bad as a milkshake.

Excellent, affirms the Admin. *Good job taking care of yourself.*

"When's the last time you had a milkshake?" asks Steve.

"I think I was probably eighteen or nineteen. I used to send my boyfriend out for one when I had cramps."

"I'm sure he galloped out to get you a milkshake too," says Steve.

"Yeah, he was a good guy."

"Well, this is an exceptional milkshake." Steve makes yummy noises at me while he takes another bite.

"I'm glad you're enjoying it. I can't afford the guilt, so have fun with that."

You are doing so well. You see? You can take care of yourself. You know what's right for you, cheers the Admin.

Why are you being so nice to me? I ask her.

You're coming back to your right mind, I can tell. Taking today off won't cost you too much, but there's some makeup work waiting – all those projects at work. People are waiting on answers from you. You held up their work today.

"What's going on?" asks Steve.

"What?"

"Looks like you have something on your mind," he tells me.

"I'm thinking about work."

"I'm sure they can go a day without you," he says, like he knows what he's saying. He doesn't.

"It just makes tomorrow harder," I explain. "I'm running analysis projects on firewall software, and I had check-in meetings today with four different teams. We're on hard deadlines to deliver and being a day behind hurts everyone, especially these days."

"Why especially these days?"

"You know, with the economy being so bad. Those of us who still have jobs feel a real need to perform at a max level every day, to prove the jobs we do are valuable and that we're good at them. I guess your work is plentiful enough that you can step away without worrying?" I ask with a snide tone, which Steve doesn't seem to hear.

"The upside of being self-employed is that I set the schedule and don't worry about getting fired," he says. "The downside is that I have to be sure I have enough contracts lined up to keep me going. Right now, I think I do."

"Good for you," I say, starting to fume.

How nice for him *that he can feel so secure,* the Admin says with a sneer.

"My husband is a contractor too," I fire at Steve. "It works for him and makes him happy, which is great, for him. My job gives us health benefits, and my steady paychecks give us security."

"Sure." Steve straightens up in his seat. He can see now he's hit a nerve with me.

"There's no guarantee, though, in being an employee," I continue. "I've seen whole teams let go in my company over the last couple of years. People who know their stuff and perform well are fired without warning. People I would think are too valuable to lose."

Could be you next, warns the Admin. *It would be hard to find another job that pays what you're earning now.*

"Sounds tough," agrees Steve again. He looks nervous as he witnesses my mounting tirade.

"My company isn't the only one, of course. Everyone everywhere is going through the same. That's what makes it scary. I can't walk away from this job or be fired in this economy." I'm ranting. "I've looked around. I've applied for other jobs. Nothing has come up, but I also wonder if I can do much better than the job I have now. There's stress in every job. Everyone I know feels overwhelmed."

"You told me this morning that you don't like what you do," Steve reminds me.

"No, I'm not passionate about software analysis, but a lot of people I work with are. They're great too. I don't want to let them down. I respect them."

"You don't share their love for this work, though," counters Steve.

"What does that matter? I'm good at what I do. My review every year is positive. I get accolades and recognition, especially from my manager, who is a supportive manager trying to grow me in my career and in the company. I have nothing to complain about," I proclaim in a raised voice as a final proof point to an argument that only exists within me. Steve waits to see if there's more. He considers what I've spouted at him.

"Sounds like you're talking yourself into being okay with where you are."

"I don't enjoy my job, but I can still be grateful for it," I say. "I can be grateful while I do analysis on software code that is beyond boring because my bills are paid. The worst, though, is having someone ask me about one of my articles and having to fake like I care to retain anything after I finish a project. The best is turning in a paper and knowing I'm done, so I can do a brain dump of everything I've learned."

"You're not happy."

"So? I would freak if I lost my job. Yes, I can feel my brain atrophy though I cram it full of data every day, and I would still freak if I lost my job." My voice is louder than I want it to be. "I would be a whole lot less happy than I am now without a job." Steve doesn't want to upset me, but he doesn't want to let me off the hook either.

"I think... I know... you can do better." Steve works to deliver this with a calm voice, hoping to calm me too.

"I work really hard." I'm about ready to cry now.

"I meant for yourself. I know you can do better for yourself."

Our sandwiches are placed before us by Alice. Neither Steve nor I look at her as we face off over my unhappiness. "Anything else I can get you?" she asks us. I can hear the tentative tone in her voice, not sure what to make of us in this moment.

"No," I say.

"No, thanks, Alice." Alice leaves us to our meal and our staring contest. Neither of us moves to eat.

"Is your life so happy?" I shoot at Steve.

"We'll get to me," he says. "Right now we're talking about you."

"I'm happy at home," I argue. "I have John and my boys. They make me happy."

"Of course they do." Then Steve stops talking. I expected him to say more, but he's not going to say what comes next.

"Then why am I here, right?" I say it for him.

"I think we're past why you're here," he corrects me. "You're here because you're unhappy. Definitely unhappy with work, and possibly unhappy with home, though you're not ready to admit it yet."

The Admin is screaming at me and at Steve, but she sounds far away. I look at Steve and find I can't argue with him anymore. "I do love them," I begin. After a breath, and then another, I continue, "I thought that having them would bring me happiness. They do and they don't. They don't make me happy… with me. I thought the life and the career would do that."

"You're not alone," Steve reassures me.

"Will I ever be happy with me?" I ask him, though I don't really expect he can answer.

"Will you ever let yourself be happy with you?"

CHAPTER 11

*S*teve and I eat our egg salad sandwiches in silence while the Admin rails at me.

What more do you think you're entitled to in this world? You're such an idiot. You have more than the majority of those walking this planet. You and your family are healthy and living well in one of the most gorgeous cities anywhere. You're selfish and ungrateful. You have family and friends and coworkers who love you and think the world of you. You are employed and earning what some would consider a ridiculous salary in an economy like we have now. You wouldn't get that salary and those benefits if you tried to get another job you might like more...

"Hi there, how's everything?" says the sweet voice of a very tall woman in a short order cook uniform standing next to our booth. She wears a red and white checked apron over her all-white clothes. She's immaculate, even though I can tell she's been cooking in the back by the smells of bacon and grill smoke that cling to her.

"Everything is delicious, thank you," says Steve. "I think this is the best egg salad sandwich I've ever had."

"I'm so glad. I'm Nellie and this is my place. It's nice to have you here."

"I really like my sandwich too, Nellie, thank you," I chime in.

"That's so good to hear, thank you. If you come back through this airport maybe you'll stop by again."

"We sure will," Steve promises, "and we'll pass on the recommendation we got to others."

"Well that's nice," says Nellie. "Someone recommended my place to you?"

"Yes," says Steve, "we came to Portland with a man out of a small town in Oregon called New Hope, in a small, ancient plane he uses to carry mail and he—"

"Ned brought you?" interrupts Nellie. "Ned is here today?" Nellie's eyes glance around the restaurant as her hands fly up to her head to check her hair. Her hands are met with the cook's hat sitting on her head. She rolls her eyes at her own awkwardness. Nellie looks around again and asks, "Is Ned joining you for lunch?"

"No, sorry," says Steve.

"Maybe he'll come in later on his own," I offer.

"Yes, he usually stops by when he's in town," Nellie tells us as her hands smooth her apron and her eyes continue to dart to the entrance.

"Have you known Ned for long?" I ask her. My curiosity is piqued. I want to know if Nellie and Ned are a hot item.

"Ned has been a regular customer and a friend for a couple of years now," says Nellie. "I suppose he recommended the egg salad sandwich to you. That's his favorite." We nod and smile at her. The nervous lift that her voice has taken on when she speaks of Ned reminds me of how I was about John in the beginning.

"Have you been for a ride in Lucy?" asks Steve. "That's a never-to-be-forgotten experience." Steve looks over to me for backup.

"I know I'll never forget it," I concur. I look up at Nellie and see that she is gazing down at me with a perturbed glint in her eye but a kind smile just the same.

" 'Fraid not," she tells me. "He hasn't asked."

"You should tell him you'd like to go for a ride," offers Steve.

"Yeah," I say, "tell him Gail and Steve recommended a ride in Lucy to you. One good recommendation deserves another." I get a sincere and full smile back from Nellie at this suggestion. She beams at the idea.

"Well, I just may do that," she says. "Thank you, Gail and Steve. It's been nice talking to you. Enjoy your lunch." Nellie gives us a final fond smile then starts back toward the kitchen. We both thank her as she goes. Just before she walks through the door to the kitchen I see her glance over at the entrance again, searching for Ned.

"How fun is that?" says Steve with an amused grin. "She really has it bad for Ned. I wonder if he knows."

"He'd have to be pretty blind not to see she likes him," I say.

"Guys can be blind," Steve says with authority. "When I met Anabeth, I was sure she was with this other guy who followed her around. Turns out he was interested in her, but she didn't feel the same. Even after I found that out, I didn't think she'd be interested in me. She told me later she liked me from the start."

"How can you think she wouldn't be interested in you? You're a nice guy, you're funny, you're very handsome – what else do you think you need to catch a girl's eye?"

"Thanks, Gail," says Steve with a grateful grin.

"John wasn't blind when we met. I had his full attention. He did everything right too, right for me anyway – like he wouldn't press me for anything. I made all the first moves. From the moment we met, we started a conversation with each other that just kept going. We emailed constantly when we weren't together. We found things to do like walk my dog or go to a movie, but we really just kept talking. There was never an awkward pause or lack of something to say." John fills my head now as I remember what a rush it was to find him.

"Sounds like he played his cards right," says Steve.

"That's just it. He didn't play a game with me. He wanted to be with me so he kept finding ways for us to get together. All I wanted was to be with him too." My mind wanders to the first time he spent the night. A smile grows from this memory and warms my face.

"What are you thinking of now?" asks Steve.

"In the very beginning, during our nonstop conversation, it got very late one night. John was at my place, and it was coming up on midnight. I didn't want him to leave, but I wasn't ready for sex, so I gave him a choice. I told him he could leave for his home or he could stay and be my pillow."

"I'm going to guess he chose pillow."

"Yes, he chose pillow." The warmth spreads from my smile down into my chest. This is one of my happiest memories. "He got into my bed fully dressed and was my pillow."

"That sounds very sweet, but it couldn't have been easy on him."

"He was a gentleman, and I do believe that's what sealed the deal. A few days later, we declared our love and after that I pounced on him."

"Nice."

"It feels special and rare these days that we said we loved each other before we made love. I don't think that happens much anymore."

"I declared my love on the wall of a bathroom stall in a club," says Steve. I give him an incredulous and confused look. "I was twenty-three and nervous and in love. Anabeth and I were at a club hanging out with friends. We'd been going out for a few weeks, and I knew I loved her. I knew I only wanted her. I just didn't know how to say it. I went to the bathroom and saw that the walls were covered in chalkboard. There were cups of chalk everywhere. I think this was the establishment's way of giving into the graffiti they knew would happen. I went into a stall and found a blank spot. I wrote, 'I love you, Anabeth.' Later in the evening she went to the bathroom – it was a unisex bathroom, which I remember being a thing in clubs in the 90s – and she just happened to use the same stall."

"Of course she did," I say.

"Of course she did. I remember her walking back from the bathroom looking straight at me. She looked fierce and sweet at the same time. She walked straight up to me and put her face about an inch away from mine. She took a breath and then whispered so only I would hear, 'I love you too.'"

"*Awwwwww.*"

"Yes, it was a very *awwwwww* moment. Much like your man pillow." We sit in our shared glow of first-love memories while we finish our lunch. I think of John and of falling in love, and I think of us now. I love him, but... what? Neither of us seems as interesting as we once were. The life and routine I craved to make me happen just feels like routine, and that includes John.

"I've been meaning to talk to you about an issue we may have," says Steve.

"Oh?" My mind remembers my lack of passport. Maybe his issue lets me off the hook of telling him I can't go on.

"The issue is Homeland Security."

"Are you telling me you're a terrorist, Steve?" Now that's a reason that would let me off the hook.

Nice joke, says the Admin, *but you don't really know this guy, do you? He told a nice story about his wife, but who knows if that's true?*

"No, Gail, I'm not a terrorist. Though, my daughter would say my cooking is torture. She's threatened to call child protective services. No, US Homeland Security is an issue for us because they've made crossing the Canadian border more difficult. We can't get over the border with just a driver's license anymore. I have a passport card I keep in my wallet." Steve reaches into his wallet and produces a card that looks like a very patriotic driver's license. It has a picture of Steve and a clear title stating that it is a United States of America Passport Card. "This gets me across the Canadian border and back again."

"I don't have a passport card," I tell him as I hand his back. Time to confess, though it doesn't feel like much of a confession since he's figured it out. "I don't have my passport with me either."

"I thought as much. I'm sorry I didn't think of this sooner. The truth is, I travel to Vancouver once a month to visit a client, so my customs paperwork and passport card are always with me."

"Really? You travel to Vancouver all the time? Well, that makes sense now. This trip seemed so easy for you. Today isn't the same grand adventure for you that it is for me."

"Today wasn't the same leap out of my comfort zone for me, no," Steve confesses, "but it has most certainly been a grand adventure – one that I'm not ready to let end. I need today as much as you do."

"It doesn't have to end for you. You have your passport card so you can keep going." There's hurt in my voice. I can hear it and so can Steve. I can see how it wounds him. At the same time, the Admin is already calculating the cost of a plane ticket home and telling me I'll need to shop for dinner when I land in San Francisco. She's smug. It's strange how her smugness is also a comfort. She always knows what should happen next.

Steve takes a deep breath and reaches his hand across the table. He lets it rest a few inches in front of me with his palm up and open. I know he feels bad for this impasse, so I take his hand and squeeze it. "It's okay," I tell him. "I'm honestly okay. I've had the most amazing morning, and now I can get home in time for the kids like we first planned."

"I want you to keep going," Steve announces. "I don't want to go without you. In fact, I won't go without you."

"I can't get across the border, Steve. What's more, if I did somehow get across, I know I couldn't get back into the States. Becoming a fugitive in the eyes of Homeland Security is not the right path for me. If we get caught, then I'm royally screwed because I do not look good in orange."

"Please don't go home yet. I know we can figure something out. Everything has worked out so far today."

"I'm not going to break the law." I start to pull my hand away from his, but he tightens his grip to try to hold it there. I start to get frustrated, so he lets me go. We both fall back against our bench seats with a loud, defeated thud.

"Uh-oh," we hear Nellie say as she approaches us. "Did something go wrong with the egg salad?"

"No," I tell her. "The sandwich was delicious."

"Phew! I'm glad to hear it. I pride myself on that sandwich. I've won a ribbon for it in the last two state fairs." We both give her half-hearted smiles. "Is there anything I can do to help you folks?"

"Do you know a way we can sneak into and out of Canada in the next twelve hours?" Steve asks her. How could he ask her that? My eyes are wide and laser-focused at his mouth to get it to close. He makes a point of not looking at me by shifting his body so he faces

Nellie. I try to kick him under the table, but he dodges my feet somehow.

"You want to sneak into and then back out of Canada in the next twelve hours?" Nellie repeats this to be sure she heard us right. "Why?"

"There's a Celebration of Light fireworks festival happening tonight. We have tickets. I have a passport card, but Gail doesn't have her passport with her," says Steve.

"Well that is rotten luck," says Nellie. She looks over at me. The mortified expression on my face hasn't lessened any since Steve started telling her everything. She considers me for a moment and then starts to giggle. Nellie tries to stifle her laughter, but it makes its way through anyway. Unable to be kept in, a series of giggles come out of Nellie as she continues to look straight at me. "Sorry about this, but your face is priceless. You look like the FBI is outside this restaurant right now, waiting to take you away for even thinking of crossing the border without a passport." Steve glances over at me and looks as though he may laugh himself, but the hard stare I give him cuts him off with no trouble. Instead, he swallows hard to clear the offending frog of humor from his throat. A small croak escapes anyway.

"Scooch over," Nellie tells Steve. Surprised, Steve looks up at Nellie with a question in his face. She waves her hand to illustrate that he should move down the bench, which he does. Nellie sits and looks straight into my eyes. She sits there for a few moments, thinking something through while she considers me. "Why is this fireworks festival important to you?" Nellie asks me.

I take a breath and think through her question. I take another breath to think through my answer. I look over at Steve, who looks as though he has his answer ready should Nellie want to ask him too. I look down at the table, checking to see if maybe the appropriate answer is written there. It's not, so I decide to tell the truth.

"I'm not happy, in general. Today has been different, though. We've been on a journey, an adventure, and it's been terrific so far. It's been exciting and it's been scary. Now I want to go home to my family, and could easily get on a plane and have the day end here." I look over at

Steve, whose eyes seem to crumple when he hears this. "But, if I'm really honest, I think I want to keep going. I know I should be filled-up happy with all that I've gotten to do today, but I'm pretty sure it would make me unhappy to stop here." Steve's smile returns. My wanting to continue perks him up. I'm terrified at the thought. "I can't break the law. I already feel terrible for stepping so far away from my family and my life. If I go further and end up in jail…" My voice trails off. I'm not sure what else to say.

"Why do you feel so bad taking a day away from your family and your life?" Nellie asks me.

"I love them, and they need me. They're all I do each day because it takes all of me to keep our life going. I look after them and take care of them – my family, my projects at work, and my house. But yes, yes, I know they'll survive without me for a day – you don't have to say it."

"Looks like you're finding out how you survive for a day without them," observes Nellie. Her words land hard in me. She can't be right. How can I be the one left flailing if I step away from my life and my responsibilities for a day? It's everyone else who will fall apart, not me.

The cleanup and catch-up tomorrow is huge. Don't listen to her. She doesn't know what it takes to run your life. The Admin gives Nellie the stink eye while she spouts words I've heard all too often. I was so sure five minutes ago those words were true. Now I wonder. Am I so essential that life crumbles when I'm away for a day?

You're the glue that holds everyone together, the Admin declares.

I've believed that. I've believed it without question, to a point that it drives me mad trying to satisfy every detail in every day because no one does all those details better than me. Listening to myself and the Admin now, however, makes it all sound kind of arrogant.

Nellie turns to Steve and asks, "What about you, Steve? Why do you need to smuggle this woman across the border to see a fireworks show with her? You have your passport card. Why not just hop on a plane now and get yourself there?"

"I hadn't told Gail this part yet," says Steve with a sideways glance in my direction. "Last night was the anniversary of the night I met my wife. My wife passed away."

"I'm so sorry," says Nellie.

"Aria, my daughter, could tell I was quiet and asked me why. I made some excuse about work. I did my best to get on with my day, just get things done. While I was getting dinner ready for us, I looked up through our kitchen window and saw this one bright star in the sky, beaming down at me through the fog. I had the idea that I should wish for something, so I wished for feelings. I know how unhappy you've been, Gail, and how that weighs on you. These days, though, instead of feeling unhappy, I don't feel. I've been numb for a long time. The grief over losing Anabeth, my wife, has short-circuited me, I think. It was too much, so I switched off. Then I got comfortable being numb. I made myself tell jokes again and be as warm as possible with Aria, but it's not the same, and I think Aria can tell. I want to start feeling again, for me and for Aria, so that's what I wished for."

"Steve," I begin.

"Let me finish, Gail. This is where you come in. I woke up this morning looking for a sign. I was ready to do something, anything, to make my wish come true. I was entertaining thoughts of quitting my job and joining the Peace Corps or doing some kind of volunteer work that would get me outside myself. All of this is going through my head when I walked into Dr. Hu's office this morning. I walked in, greeted the receptionist, then looked over and there you were sitting with a magazine in your hands. Do you remember what was on the cover of the magazine, Gail?" I shake my head no. Sitting in Dr. Hu's office feels like a distant memory now.

"You were holding a *Vanity Fair* with some young girl I didn't recognize on the cover, but the large words stacked next to her said, 'Once More with Feeling!' I didn't know if my sign today would be that blatant, but I knew I had to introduce myself to you and see what happened next. Now here we are."

We all sit in silence for a few moments, taking this story in. It seems surreal that his wish on a star set this whole series of events in motion.

Nellie breaks the silence. "You two just met this morning?" Her voice is incredulous.

"Yes," I tell her. "It's hard for me to believe too."

"This is a quest. You're both on a quest. I can get behind a quest," announces Nellie. "As it turns out, you folks had the right egg salad sandwich in the right restaurant today. I know exactly how you can get across the border and back."

CHAPTER 12

*H*alf-crazed with doubt and worry, John is flying around his house trying to do three things at once: find babysitting for the boys, book an airline ticket to Portland, and pack. Multitasking is new to John. The frantic pace required to do all three at once is just making him, well, frantic. Instead, John uses a trick he sees Gail use when she's like this. He makes a list on the kitchen whiteboard so he can focus on one task at a time.

1. Babysitting for the boys. John doesn't want to explain to Gail's parents what he doesn't understand about Gail's whereabouts or the one-way plane ticket he's about to buy. John decides to call friends instead of family. John calls their friend Eric, who has boys about the same age as Zach and Damon. On the phone, John tells him that he's planning a surprise for Gail – somewhat true – and asks if Eric could take the boys in for a sleepover at the last minute. Eric is more than happy to help and knows that his boys will be thrilled. Phew, one thing done. John will pack the boys a small bag and drop it and the car seats off at Eric's house on his way to the airport. John erases babysitting off the white board.

2. Buying a plane ticket to Portland. John comes to a sudden halt. What if this is all okay and not the threatening situation he fears?

Before he spends hundreds of dollars on a ticket, maybe he should just call Gail and ask her to explain. John takes out his phone and checks the locator service. Gail's dot has moved across the airport to the main terminal. John stops breathing. Where is she now? A tag appears above where Gail's dot is sitting in the terminal. It reads "Nellie's Sandwich Shack." She's getting lunch, thinks John. How nice for her. I'm going out of my mind, and she's probably sitting there enjoying her sandwich.

For a few moments, John doesn't move. He doesn't want to think the worst, but he has to admit, at least to himself, that he's angry. He's here and she's there and he doesn't know why. If things were okay, then she would have told him she was going to Portland, right? Maybe he should just let her go and see what she does. No, he'll go nuts waiting for her to call or come home. He has to do something.

John goes to his computer and pulls up a website for cheap airplane tickets. He finds a flight that leaves in two hours and books it. He erases airplane ticket off the white board. Two hours feels like an eternity to John. He needs to keep moving, just keep moving with what comes next.

3. Pack. John starts thinking of what to pack for himself and then for the boys. He figures he should pack a couple of changes of clothes for himself in a backpack. He wants to stay light. He doesn't know what is going to happen today as he hunts down his wife. Then a thought occurs to him that shoots a harpoon of fear straight at John's heart. He can hear it whistling toward him. He rushes to his bedroom and throws open a small top drawer of a bureau he and Gail share. John lets out a long breath of relief when he sees there are four passports in the drawer. Gail didn't take her passport. John would like to think that's a good sign. She's not leaving the country. He looks through the four passports and finds his and Gail's. Last week they talked about planning a vacation. Gail has a lot of vacation days accrued. John suggested the Caribbean or Costa Rica, somewhere warm where they could relax together. It doesn't feel like they relax together much anymore. He even said as much to Gail, but she was distracted with a work email and didn't hear him.

John puts his and Gail's passports in his jacket pocket. He doesn't know what's about to happen, but the feel of the passports against his heart causes both hope and fear to course through John. For the moment, the harpoon is deflected. His heart is beating hard, yet there's a comfort in the hope it carries.

"I'll take the passports so if Gail needs to get away, I can go with her." John says his wish aloud, hoping some angel is listening. The wish is followed by a thought that he doesn't want to voice: *unless what she needs is to get away from me.*

CHAPTER 13

"*I*'m making a run for the border with a man I met this morning," I say out loud. If I keep it inside, then the Admin will need to comment.

"Kind of freaky, isn't it?" says Steve. "It's freaky, I think, because it feels like I'm exactly where I need to be right now. How about you? Do you feel like you're where you should be – here in this rented car with a crazy plan to cross the Canadian border illegally with a man who could still be considered a stranger since you've only known him for six hours?"

"Has it really been just six hours?" I ask.

"Yep."

"That is freaky. The rest is freaky too, just like you said. I'm still freaked out by today and the fact that I continue to go along with this ride. But," I pause to consider what I'm about to say, wanting to be sure it's true, "I'm glad I'm here. I'm glad I didn't get on a plane to go home."

"Me too," says Steve, and he is sincere. I can hear his sincerity in those two small words. After our talk with Nellie, I understand how important this journey is to him. I also see how important it is to him that I'm here, though I'm still not sure why. Maybe it's to bear witness.

If he ever has doubts in the days and years to come about today and all that happened, he'll have me as assurance that today was real. Maybe he doesn't know yet himself why he needs me here.

He doesn't need you, says the Admin from the back seat of the car. Even if he thinks he does, you could disappear and it wouldn't matter. You should disappear. How can you say you're glad to be here? What does that say about the past few years of your life? This pointless trip to see a fireworks show has become more important to you than your family and the job that supports your family.

I wish I could hate you, I whisper through thick anger to her. I don't like you.

I don't care that you don't like me. You need me. You know you need me to keep you straight. Liking me doesn't matter.

Why can't today be good for me? I implore. Shouldn't I get to do something for myself?

You're a failure for not doing something for yourself that keeps you honest with John and your boss.

Like what? Get my nails done? See a movie alone?

What will you tell Zach and Damon about today? needles the Admin. That it's okay to lie as long as you think the lie is good for you?

That isn't fair.

It's your rule that you made. There will be a price for breaking your own rule. Bull's-eye. The Admin hits the center of my fear: there will be a penalty I have to pay for today, as sure as I'm sitting here. I've enjoyed myself too much.

"You're quiet again," Steve tells me. "I get nervous when you're quiet."

"Why?" I ask him.

"Your mood takes a downward turn, for some reason."

"Hmm, that makes sense," I say.

"What are you thinking?" Steve asks.

"I'm wondering how I'm going to explain this day to my boys. How I skipped out of town, didn't tell Daddy, and did crazy things for no good reason."

"There's a good reason," says Steve. "You may not see it yet, but there's a good reason or you wouldn't be here."

"What if it's a bad reason?" I ask.

"I've only known you a few hours, but I can say with a high degree of certainty that I think you're here for a good reason."

"Are you saying you know why I'm here?" I ask Steve, hoping he does know and can tell me.

"I don't know all the details of what brought you here, but I think the simple truth is that you're here because you need to be. You're doing this trip for you – to bring some living back into your life." Steve opens his mouth to say more, but he hesitates before he speaks. "I'm here for me too, to take care of me." I guess he's figuring out today as he goes too.

"It's possible that we're doing something for ourselves that isn't good for us," I suggest to see what he thinks. "Maybe it just feels good, like doing heroin."

"Have you done heroin?" asks Steve.

"No! I have not done heroin. What kind of question is that?"

"You brought up heroin like you knew what you were saying, so I asked."

"I was using it as a metaphor, duh! Everyone knows that heroin must feel really good or people wouldn't throw their lives away using it all the time. Do I look like someone who would take heroin to you?"

"You didn't strike me as someone who would say 'duh,' but you just did. Like, I haven't had someone say 'duh' to me since the '80s, like okay?" Steve puts on a Valley girl tone with this last line.

It's too much. I erupt with laughter. This could be a big one. Volume rises with the flow of my guffawing. It feels good. I want to let loose with this powerful laugh of mine. I decide to let it happen. I throw my head back to give air and space to what must now be jettisoned from the extra laugh organ I'm sure my body has that most others do not possess. The laughter fills the car in an instant. Somewhere a small thought occurs to me that I should roll down my window so the echoing force of my laugh doesn't deafen Steve, but I don't want to do anything now but laugh, so that's what I do.

I lose track of time when I'm laughing like this. Seconds or minutes later, I start to calm down. I look over at Steve, who has a grin on his face like the Cheshire Cat. This makes me want to laugh more, but I've gone on long enough. I don't want to end up scaring Steve, make him think I'm losing it, plus my side is starting to hurt. I try to calm myself down again. Steve, however, isn't ready for the laughter to stop.

"Like, your laugh is bitchin' loud!" says Valley girl Steve. There it is. The laughter starts rolling hard again. "Tubular!" Steve screams over me. "Like, this is totally blowing my mind."

"Stop!" I manage to eject this one word out in between bursts of laughter.

"But your laugh is so rad!" An image of Steve in acid-washed jeans with holes in the knees, white sneakers, and a slashed, sleeveless KISS T-shirt leaps into my head. Now it's serious – the laughter is causing me serious pain in my side. I curl up, bringing my knees to my chest while digging my fist into my waist.

"Are you okay?" Steve asks in between giggles of his own.

"My side," I squeak out in between laughs. "Please stop," I plead with him.

"Okay, okay." Steve lets me off the hook.

It takes me a while to calm down. The stitch in my side lessens. When I'm able to stretch my legs out again and stop digging my fist into my side, I heave a large contented sigh of relief. Dr. Cackle has turned back into Mrs. Harker. Steve remains quiet, bless him, while the laugh juices retreat back to the organ from whence they came. The ringing subsides from my ears, and my head is clear. In fact, my head is crystal clear, like the sky the day after a hard rain. I turn to Steve to share this and see that he's deep in his own world of thought. While his mood doesn't look sour like mine tends to become when I retreat inside myself, he does look concerned.

"What are you thinking?" I ask him.

"I'm running through Nellie's instructions on how to find this place," he tells me. "They seem easy, but I wonder if they're too easy and we're walking into something that she doesn't know is waiting, like a border patrol or a cousin with a shotgun."

"It does seem unreal that this passage would remain hidden this whole time. For gossip reasons alone, you'd think someone would have talked about it," I say.

"It's probably going to be okay. This place is out in the middle of nowhere along the Canadian border," Steve reasons, "and those who used it during Prohibition have passed away."

"Those people had kids, though, and grandkids like Nellie," I say. "Someone had to brag about how they ran rum into the United States from Canada, or how their parents ran rum."

"Maybe they were protecting themselves and their families. Maybe they didn't name Nellie's granddad when they told their stories because his land could have been taken away, who knows?" says Steve.

"Yeah, maybe," is all I can think to say, so I change the subject. "Six hours since this day began." I look at the digital clock on the car dashboard. It reads 2:16. "My kids are finishing their school day. They go into an after-care program next. It'll be another three hours before they know I'm gone – not home, I mean."

My phone rings. I look down and see that John is calling me. Steve looks down at my phone and sees the picture of John that has appeared in my screen. In the picture, John is blowing me a kiss.

"John is calling you," Steve announces, like I didn't know.

"Yes."

"Are you going to answer it?" he asks.

"I don't know what to say," I tell him.

"Say hello."

I give it some thought, then I decide to answer John's call. I move my finger to press 'Answer' but the ringing stops. I wait to see if he leaves a message. I wait. No message. "He didn't leave a message," I tell Steve. "I guess it wasn't that important."

"Maybe he just wanted to hear your voice," says Steve. "That's important."

"You think I should call him back?" I ask.

"I don't know what to tell you," says Steve. "Yes, I think you should call him, and no I don't want you to call and then abandon the mission."

"We're on a mission?"

"Yes, we're on a mission from God," says Steve in an affected accent I don't recognize. "We're 106 miles from Vancouver. We got a full tank of gas, half a pack of gum, it's a bright afternoon, and we're not wearing sunglasses." Steve looks at me like he's waiting for something. Then he says, "Come on! You were supposed to say, 'Hit it'."

"Hit what?" I ask.

"I was Elwood Blues and you're supposed to be Jake Blues sitting next to me in the car and... never mind. Call your husband. If he asks what you're doing, tell him you're on a mission from God."

I look at my phone and consider calling John. Again, I can't fathom how to explain this day to him when I can't explain it to myself. I put the phone back in my purse. I look over at Steve, whose eyebrows are raised like question marks high above his eyes. "I'll call him after we cross the border," I explain. "Hopefully, not from jail."

CHAPTER 14

I want to call back, thinks John. *I should call back. I need to talk to her. I need to hear her voice. What if she says she's leaving me? Then I'll know. Then I won't be in another state chasing after her when I could be home while my world is shredded into pieces.*

John checks the locator service again. Gail's dot is in Washington state and is moving north.

"Now what?" says John out loud.

"Now you need to turn off your phone please so we can take off," says a flight attendant over John's shoulder. He stares after the attendant who is moving forward along the airplane aisle checking that everyone is stowed, secure, compliant, and not panicking. *I feel like panicking,* thinks John. *Maybe if I panic, they'll throw me off the plane and I can call Gail again.*

"I'm not sure I believe that it makes a difference, but you should probably turn the phone off. That attendant doesn't look like she's having a great day," says the passenger next to John.

John looks down at his phone. He's stuck in an honest fight-or-flight moment. Does he fight his way off the plane to make his phone call or take the flight to chase his wife?

"She's eyeing you," says the voice to John's left. John looks up to see the flight attendant's suspicious stare. She starts moving back toward him. John sees the airplane doors have been sealed shut and that the plane is about to start taxiing down the runway. He takes a breath and chooses flight. He doesn't know how he's supposed to find Gail now, but he turns off his phone and stows it in his pocket just as the attendant reaches him. She gives him a quick scan for illegal activity and then floats by without missing a step.

"Thank you for the warning," says John as he looks to the man on his left. "I'm John."

"Edgar, and you're welcome. To be honest, I didn't want the plane to be delayed by your phone call."

"Right, sorry," says John.

"No need to apologize. It looked like an important call. Still, I didn't want the flight attendant coming down on you and delaying us. She looks primed for a power trip. I trust no one is dying?"

Just my soul, thinks John.

"Oh God! Is someone dying, and I made you put your phone away?" asks Edgar.

"No, no one is dying," says John. "I'm not sure what's happening right now in my life, but I'm pretty sure no one is dying."

"Okay," says Edgar, relieved. "Well, what's happening right now is that you're on a plane to Portland sitting next to San Francisco's premiere crepes maker." Edgar straightens himself up as tall as he can in his seat. "I am the Crepes Fairy!" With this, Edgar pulls back the left side of his jacket to reveal an ornate fairy broach pinned above his heart. The fairy, wearing a chef's hat that sparkles, holds a tiny pan.

"I've heard of you," says John. "You have a restaurant on Valencia, right?"

"That's right," says the Crepes Fairy. "Have you been?"

"Not yet, but I keep meaning to mention it to my wife. I'm sure my kids would love it too."

"Kids can't get enough of my crepes. I have a dynamite kids' menu. To start, I make crepes shaped like sticks of dynamite. The favorite for kids is the Kermit crepe, though. It's green." Edgar pauses for effect.

He loves how this fact stuns people. "True to Kermit's song, it isn't easy being green, but very popular."

"You just use food coloring, right?" asks John.

"No, that's the best part. It's spirulina and pureed spinach. The kids have no idea how healthy they're eating. They just love that it's green and shaped like Kermit."

"That's incredible," says John with the right amount of awe. Edgar is pleased.

"It's fun," says Edgar. "It's what I love to do. I'm also pretty good at telling which of my crepes a person should try. Watching your face after you hung up your phone made me think that the 'I Left My Heart in San Francisco' crepe would be the one for you today. It isn't a very pretty crepe, but I don't think art has to be what we traditionally deem beautiful. Beauty can be found in places that disturb us too."

"What does the 'I Left My Heart in San Francisco' crepe look like?" John asks.

"It's shaped like a heart – a real heart, not a Valentine heart – and it's blood red. I make it with a base of beet paste to give it that deep color and a slightly bitter bite. Over it, I pour a thick syrup of raspberry reduction that is infused with vanilla to deepen its color too. For effect, I rip the heart open so there's a jagged tear into its middle. The rip makes it look like the syrup flows from the heart itself."

Edgar's delight grows as he describes each new facet of his creation to John. By the time he's finished, Edgar's giddiness is as bright as a halogen light bulb. John's mind leaps to the black-and-white movie in which Dr. Frankenstein exclaims, 'It's alive!'

"Edgar, I am impressed, and kind of scared. I think I would order one right now," admits John.

"Told you," says Edgar. "Crepes are my life, and knowing which crepe is right for a person is part of my gift."

"My face made you think I should have the bloody heart crepe?" asks John.

"Honey, heartache is an easy read," says Edgar. "I could tell when you walked onto the plane that your heart was hurt. Whatever that little locator dot that you checked when you sat down told you seemed to tear you open."

"I should have checked it before I boarded the plane," says John. "Might have saved me a trip."

"Do you mind me asking who the dot is?" Edgar inquires.

"My wife."

"Ouch, that does hurt," says Edgar. "I guess she's not where you thought she would be?"

"No."

"Sorry," Edgar offers.

"No need to apologize, but thanks."

"Were you supposed to meet her in Portland?" asks Edgar.

"No, I was supposed to see her back home after her dentist's appointment this morning. Instead, she texts me saying she's taking the day off for herself and I'd see her tonight, which is great. She never takes a break. I was happy for her. Then she calls and tells me she's going to be out late, and I shouldn't wait up for her. Still fine, I'm still happy for her. Then I had a question for her about the shower after we hung up, so I looked up her location to be sure I wasn't disturbing her in the middle of a movie and..." John doesn't know how to finish the sentence, and doesn't want to try.

"And *wham!* You discover she's in Portland?" asks Edgar.

"Yes, especially the *wham* part," says John.

"I'm not sure what to say."

"Me either," agrees John.

"You're going after her."

"Yes."

"Does she know you're coming?" asks Edgar.

"No," says John. "She didn't tell me what she's doing, and I didn't know how to tell her I was coming after her. Now her dot is in Washington state and is moving north."

"What's north?" asks Edgar.

"I have no idea," says John.

"Is there family up north? Or a friend?" asks Edgar.

"No." John looks to Edgar, hoping he can make sense of it all.

Maybe a stranger can see something he doesn't. "She didn't take her passport with her. I have it with me."

"Okay, so she's not leaving the country, that's good," says Edgar. "Why did you bring her passport?"

"If she really needs to go somewhere, I'm hoping I'll get to go too, but I won't hold her back either."

Edgar's right hand covers his heart as he heaves an audible sigh. "John, you have just won me over. I can't imagine your wife saying no to a heart like yours. How did you two meet?"

"We met at a party in San Francisco. I happened to be dating a girl she went to high school with, but this other girl and I were on the tail end of our run together. She was also in the middle of a break-up with the last guy she dated. My girlfriend and I got separated during the party. When I found her, my girlfriend was talking with her. Just as I walk up, I hear my girlfriend say, 'Don't be sad. Kiss John. John will make you feel better.' I think that was my clue from her that we were about done, but I look over and there's this cute girl in dungarees looking up at me with shock at my girlfriend's suggestion. The look on her face alone was enough to make me want to kiss her, and the fact that she was so pretty didn't hurt. It was intense too, how pretty she was to me. I leaned over and kissed her. She kissed me back. It wasn't a long kiss, but it was enough. My girlfriend excused herself to find the next guy, and my future wife and I found a place to sit and talk."

"Did you smooch her again?" asks Edgar.

"Not that night, no, we just sat and talked and ignored everyone else," says John.

"How long have you been together?" asks Edgar.

"Fifteen years. We have two kids," says John who knew the next question would be about kids. John waits, but Edgar doesn't ask anything more. "Have you run out of things to ask about my runaway wife, Edgar?"

"Sorry, I'm not sure what else to ask about your runaway wife."

"Sure you do, go ahead," prompts John. "It's the logical next question to ask about why my wife is hundreds of miles away and didn't tell me what she's doing."

"Do you think she's seeing someone?" asks Edgar. The pain of the question spoken aloud allows the harpoon of fear, deflected before, to hit its mark in John's chest. The small shield of hope that protected his heart is gone. He hadn't dared ask himself this. This was not an option he could explore on his own.

"John, are you okay? You don't have to answer that," offers Edgar.

"I don't know," John replies. "I don't want to think so. I can't think of anything she did before today that would tell me she's seeing someone."

"Well, let that question go for now then. Deal with it if it comes up, otherwise let it go. No use winding yourself up when you don't know," instructs Edgar, trying to make this moment easier on John.

"You're right." John tries to do as Edgar suggests and relax, but the harpoon is fixed in its place. "What am I doing? I'm chasing after her. If she wanted me with her, then I'd be with her, right?" Edgar doesn't answer. "I couldn't just sit at home and wait for the news. I had to do something." John's stomach rumbles loudly enough for Edgar and the passengers across the aisle to hear. "Sorry, I could use that bloody crepe about now."

"I guess food wasn't a high priority for you today," says Edgar.

"I guess not. Though, my wife was able to sit and have lunch. Food wasn't an issue for her." John can hear the bitterness creeping into his voice. "She ate at a place in the Portland airport called Nellie's Sandwich Shack for lunch, according to her dot."

"Of course she did," says Edgar. "Nellie makes the best sandwiches. You should save your appetite and get a sandwich at her place."

The flight attendant appears next to John with the cart of in-flight food. "I'm not sure I can last that long," he says to Edgar. "I'll get a ham sandwich here."

"Don't eat the whole thing. Trust me. Eat half and then order a ham sandwich from Nellie. She makes a ham sandwich that will curl your toes and make you want to sing."

The bread on the plane's sandwich is dry, making it easy for John to only eat half. A cup of coffee later and a fog seems to clear from his brain.

"Why are you going to Portland, Edgar?" asks John.

"I needed to get out of the city for a few days. I have family in Portland," answers Edgar, who suddenly seems to John like he has his own heartache he's dealing with.

"When we land, can you point me in the direction of Nellie's Sandwich Shack? I want to see if there's anything I can find out there before I try to call my wife again," John explains.

"I'll do better than that," says Edgar. "I'll walk you to Nellie's myself. I told you I go there every time I'm in Portland. I'm going to buy you her ham sandwich so you taste for yourself how wrong you were to waste good stomach space on airplane food. I'm also interested in helping you. I like to believe that happy endings happen and love prevails. If not for me, then for someone nice like you."

CHAPTER 15

*J*ohn and Edgar both leave the plane with a carry-on.

"Do you have checked baggage you need to pick up?" ask John.

"No, my flight today was a last minute decision," says Edgar as they enter the airport through gate 17. Edgar takes the lead since he knows where they're going. John is grateful that for the next few minutes he's following a helpful stranger instead of chasing his absent wife.

"How last minute?" asks John.

Edgar looks at his watch. "By my calculations, I bought my ticket four hours ago."

"Huh, I bought mine a little after you. Hopefully your last minute travel reason is better than mine."

"I don't know. I watched others leave this morning for a day trip adventure. I would have given away ten secret crepes recipes to go. I tried my best to be happy for them and ended up in a sullen, jealous place. I was in the middle of devising how to make a poison apple crepe when I decided it might be best that I leave town."

Edgar's pace quickens then, and John lets the conversation drop. As they briskly walk through the Portland airport, John looks around for anything interesting to distract him. Either his mind can't focus enough to find something, or his eyes are terrible at looking. The Portland airport looks like any other airport – a large, sterile waiting room. It has a scattering of Portland tchotchkes that may set it apart, but the shops, eateries, strategically placed restrooms, and the boarding areas filled with people ready to move but having to sit scream at John from every angle. This is a place of transition, and Gail was here.

Terminal is an unfortunate word that doesn't fit this place, thinks John. Everything here is about moving people to somewhere else. John knows Gail has left the airport. Still, his eyes scan the corridors and the shops for signs of her. John pays particular attention to the bookstores and shops with toys. These are the places Gail usually stops for a magazine and something for the kids. He wonders if she bought the kids something while she was here. The thought of her buying toys makes the pilot light of fear in John's stomach ignites his anger once again. Is she thinking of their kids? Is she thinking through what an absent Mom will do to them?

Edgar, meanwhile, is making small talk while pointing out eateries and newsstands he recommends over others in the airport. He even waves to a few people along the way who are working in them. "That's Carol," says Edgar, pointing to a woman standing behind a bar and then waving at her. "She mixes the best Long Island Iced Teas, but her whiskey always tastes a little watered down to me."

"You really seem to know this place. I guess you visit home often?" asks John.

"Yeah, something like that."

Two minutes later, they turn a corner and John sees the diner. For a moment, it sparkles at him like found treasure. In the next moment, the smoldering harpoon in John's chest reminds him that Gail was here, and it could be she wasn't alone.

Edgar starts to sprint to the open entrance of Nellie's Sandwich Shack. His final steps are more like bounces that land him a few feet into the middle of the diner, surrounded by tables of people eating. John wonders what has gotten into Edgar. Can the sandwiches here be that good?

With great aplomb, Edgar strikes a superhero pose with his hands on his hips, his legs spread in a sturdy stance, his chest out, and his chin high. "I seek the lady of this fine establishment!" bellows Edgar. "She whose Greek Pita has tempted the Gods, whose Italian Meatball has left Sicilians weeping, and whose fresh homemade focaccia is known in lands both far and near."

John hasn't had a Crepes Fairy crepe, but he thinks Edgar has missed his calling. There are stages and theaters in New York and London missing this star who stands in a shiny diner in Portland.

"Come forth, sweet Nellie! Thou titan of bready products!"

John watches as a tall lady dressed in a crisp cook's outfit with a name tag that reads "Nellie" bursts from the kitchen door wielding a soup ladle. She strikes a pose similar to Edgar's but holds the soup ladle high above her head like a scepter or a sword. With a voice to match the volume and timbre of Edgar's, Nellie replies, "What manner of miscreant dares disturb me whilst I create magnificent morsels for these fine patrons?"

"We are weary travelers, madam, who seek nourishment and guidance along our way. I bring with me a man on a noble quest." Edgar indicates John with a flourish of his hand. "He has queries that he must make of you, while we fill ourselves here on the manna from heaven you do conjure." Nellie looks John over with a leery eye. She even sneers at him a little. John hopes this is part of the act. "Though I know it has been a long while since our last meeting, I hope thou will have some recollection of me, dear lady," Edgar prompts.

Nellie marches over to Edgar and stops directly in front of him. She is head and shoulders taller than he is and looks down at him with suspicion. "You do look familiar. Something in the eyes and curve of your nose reminds me of a man I once knew. A man who also revels in the bready arts as I do."

" 'Tis I! I am that man – who is your brother." Edgar and Nellie both pause for dramatic effect before they break out into wide grins and give each other a big hug. For a moment, John thinks Nellie even lifts Edgar from the floor a centimeter or two. Smiling customers giggle and even offer some applause. The siblings bow to the crowd before wandering stage right toward John.

"You could have warned me you were coming," says Nellie to Edgar. "I'd have made my ambrosia for you." Nellie stops walking for a moment to look Edgar over. "You're not wearing your fairy tights?"

"I left my tights in San Francisco, along with my heart, but that's another story," says Edgar. "I'm sorry I didn't call. It was a last minute decision to come." Edgar gestures over to John again. "Come meet my new friend, John."

Nellie walks over to John and shakes his hand. "Hi John, I'm Nellie."

"Hi Nellie," replies John as he looks from Nellie to Edgar and back again.

"You're wondering how a tall, sleek, Amazon-like blonde can be the sister of this hairy, squat, swarthy man, right?" Nellie asks.

"I hate when you call me squat," mumbles Edgar.

"I know," says Nellie in response, then turns her attention back to John. "Our parents found each other and married when I was five and Edgar was eight." Nellie puts an arm around Edgar's shoulders and stands straight as a board to illustrate her height. "I'm Edgar's little sister," says Nellie with a look of pride.

"I also hate when you do this," an embarrassed Edgar mumbles again.

"I know," says Nellie smugly. "Come in and have a seat, guys." Nellie leads them to a booth in her establishment. Edgar and John sit opposite each other while Nellie remains standing. "What can I get you to drink?"

"Is there fresh orange juice left?" asks Edgar.

"There is, and for you, John?"

"Black coffee please," says John.

"Coming right up." Nellie gives Edgar a quick wink before walking away.

Edgar leans back into his booth and relaxes, looking content like one settled into an old familiar chair. John likes that Edgar looks happy, though he himself is leaning forward with his elbows on the table, hands clasped with anxiety.

"That was quite the entrance," says John.

"Thank you. I was a drama major." Edgar soaks up the praise like all good actors. "We've always had fun play-acting together. I was hoping to impress you with our theatrics, so I kept the sibling fact to myself. I'm glad it worked."

"Did you grow up in Portland?" John inquires, though making small talk seems to cause the harpoon in his chest to twist. John wants to get down to business and question Nellie.

"For the most part, yes," Edgar responds. "John, you look like you're about to jump out of your skin. Take a slow breath. Nellie will be back in a moment."

John does his best to breathe. He notices his shoulders are next to his ears and concentrates on bringing them down below his neck where they belong.

CHAPTER 16

"We're closing in on the border," Steve tells me. He's checking a map on his smart phone while I drive. "In about an hour is when we'll start seeing the landmarks Nellie told us to follow to get to her family place."

"We still have a ways to go then," I say.

"We'll be there quicker than you think," Steve replies.

The thought doesn't do me much good. I'm about to cross an international border without my passport. I'll break federal laws. I'll be a felon. Worse, it flies in the face of Homeland Security. I'll have a criminal record with the same department that tracks terrorists. My stomach twists up and clamps itself to my ribs. My ears start to burn as my anxiety pushes blood up into my head like a rising lava flow. These things I can handle. They're commonplace to me. Anxiety happens almost daily at work when I'm meeting deadlines from a dozen people, or when I'm working at home meeting my own weekend deadlines of what has to be accomplished around the house before the work week starts again. The one I can't ignore is the ocular migraine I get when my stress is through the roof like it is now.

A band of light develops across my left eye, blocking about 30 percent of my vision. I can still see well enough, but I know the band of light will grow brighter to the point of making me legally blind before it goes away. I can't continue to drive and must pull over. I have to tell Steve. It feels like a failure, a weakness.

It's a flag, chirps the Admin. *You won't listen to me, so your body is stopping you in your tracks.*

I know the migraine will go away, and that it won't cause me pain. My vision is the only impairment the ocular migraines bring on. Still, it isn't safe for me to drive. "I have to pull over," I say to Steve as calmly as I can.

"Are you okay?" asks Steve.

I pull the car to the side of the freeway on a wide shoulder that puts us far enough away from the traffic barreling past us. I turn the car off and slump back in my seat with my eyes closed. "I'm having an ocular migraine. It'll go away in a few minutes. I just have to close my eyes, breathe, and relax. I can still drive. I just need five or ten minutes. I'll be okay." I can hear the strain in my voice, and I wonder if Steve can too. I don't want to be a disappointment this far into our journey.

You were a disappointment when you left the house this morning, pokes the Admin from the back seat. *There were a number of things on your list you were supposed to do before leaving for the dentist today that you didn't do. That was disappointing enough – now look at where you are.*

"Gail, why did you go to breakfast with me this morning?" asks Steve.

Tell him the truth, instructs the Admin. *Tell him you, a married woman, thought he was hot. Tell him how you ignored your husband, your work, your oral hygiene, and followed him out of that dentist office because your hormones told you to.*

"I don't know why," I tell Steve.

"Can you try to remember?" Steve prods. "What was going through your head? Why did you accept an impromptu breakfast date from a stranger?"

Tell him, says the Admin.

"I was flattered. You're good-looking, and you were asking me to have breakfast with you." I keep my tone flat, trying to curb the embarrassment, but I can feel the blush rise in my face. I bring a hand up over my eyes. It doesn't matter that they're already closed. It helps to mask my shame.

"That's flattering to hear," says Steve, "but I'm going to guess that it was more than how I look. Think back," he tells me. "Think back to this morning, or last night, or some time before we met when you thought or said or wished for something that could make you get up and go have breakfast with me today."

My hand slides off my face and back into my lap. My eyes remain closed. My own words come back to me like a flashing neon sign in my head. Maybe it's the ocular migraine that makes them so bright. No, it's the sudden understanding of the power those words had. "I did wish," I tell Steve. "I made a wish as I walked out of my house this morning. It was small. No one heard it but me."

I heard it, the Admin complains.

"What did you wish?" asks Steve.

It was a selfish wish. You're a failure for wishing it, proclaims the Admin.

I open my eyes and look at Steve. The band of light stretches over his head like a halo. "I wished for magic. I wanted to see magic in my life again."

Steve smiles. "Your wish came true."

I smile back, "It did." The smile slides from my face, though, when I think of what comes next. I'm going to cross into Canada without a passport. I will defy the laws of my country. In this day and age, I have no illusions that the US Border Guards will go easy on me because I tell them I crossed to see a fireworks show.

"Why did you wish for magic?" Steve continues to pry. What is he after with these questions?

You're selfish and greedy and don't appreciate what you have, the Admin wants to answer for me. *Tell him that. It's the truth.*

"I don't know, Steve. I'm blessed in my life. I don't know why I would wish for more," I say, somewhat impatient now and ready for another subject.

"Is there something missing from your life?" asks Steve.

Me, is my immediate answer that I keep to myself, because it sounds pathetic.

You are pathetic, confirms the Admin. *You have more than you deserve as it is.*

"Let me ask another question," says Steve. "With all your blessings, why don't you enjoy them?"

"That feels like a loaded question, Steve, and what I don't like right now is that I don't know the answers you're pressing to hear." I'm getting snide now. The band of light across my vision increases, so I close my eyes again and try to calm down. I look for an answer that may appease him. "Maybe I need to schedule more fun in my life. Find some local trapeze artists and sign up for classes."

"Making time for fun is always a good idea," affirms Steve. "I'm glad I was there to see your first flight through the air too. Is there something you loved to do for yourself before you found the trapeze? I have a tough time seeing you leaving home to join the circus one day."

"I have a job. The trapeze would just be a hobby." I make light, hoping the conversation will shift.

"You don't like your job," Steve reminds me. "Finding something you love and doing that would probably make for a happier Gail. Have you ever found something you really love to do – no matter how ridiculous you think it is?" Steve is earnestly trying to help me, I can tell. I put my irritation at his questions in check to see if something good can come of them.

"I like making clothes for my kids," I say. "I wish I had more time for it."

You're not that good, is the Admin's opinion.

"I'm not that good," I repeat aloud.

"Do your kids wear the clothes you make?" Steve asks.

"Yes, they wear the clothes I make them. I'm their mother, so they can't say no."

"Sure they can. Even if they have to do something, kids are great about letting you know when they don't like it. Do they complain about wearing the clothes you make them?"

"No." I think back, and it occurs to me they don't complain about my clothes – and I have vocal kids.

"Do they like the clothes you make them?" Steve continues.

"I don't know, I guess they do. They sometimes make requests for custom clothes, which is fun. I like making them something I know they'll enjoy." The memories of superhero pajamas and jackets with hidden treasure pockets I've made to order spring to the forefront of my mind.

"There it is," declares Steve. "Your face lit up when you talked about making clothes that make your kids happy. Do that, at least as a start. Make time for clothes-making and see what happens. Make clothes for other kids too. When you have a bunch of clothes made, then march those kids into a local shop parading your wares and start making money."

"No way," I say.

"Why not?"

"I don't have time for that" is the handy answer I believe is true.

You don't deserve it. The Admin starts her favorite chant.

"Make time," Steve volleys back to me, unwilling to watch me make easy excuses.

"I can't imagine adding another thing to my day that I'm supposed to accomplish," I say.

You don't deserve it, chants the Admin.

"See yourself sewing, feel how happy it makes you, and then find the time," Steve says. "I'm not saying it'll be easy, but it could be rewarding. It might even be the answer for lasting happiness in your life."

You don't deserve it, chimes in the Admin.

"I'm not that good," I proclaim. "I can't imagine anyone buying my stuff."

"You don't know unless you try, and businesses don't pop up overnight. It takes dedication. You could build something solid over time." Steve is doing his best to coach me, but he doesn't get my real issue.

You don't deserve it, chants the Admin on cue.

"Find an hour or just thirty minutes tomorrow to make space for a workstation – nothing more than that. The next day, find thirty minutes more to set up your sewing machine or get yourself some materials. It won't happen overnight. In fact, if it means something to you, then it will take time to grow and develop into the designer you want to be, and that's the fun part."

You have too much going on to find three minutes for this frivolous idea, let alone thirty, says the Admin, *and you don't deserve it.*

"Yes, I do," I say out loud. Hearing my voice speak my dissent surprises both me and the Admin.

No, you don't. The Admin has had enough. She throws images across my mind of all the chores around the house I haven't finished and all the projects I've started but failed to complete. She illustrates in Technicolor shame how I haven't earned the right to do something just for fun, just for me.

"Yes you do, what?" asks Steve. I'd almost forgotten he was here.

"I was saying that I think I deserve to get to do something that makes me happy," I explain with a small voice. My confidence of just a moment ago has been cut off at the knees by the Admin.

"Of course, you do." Steve's affirmation is loud like a cheer. I open my eyes to see that he believes it. He sees me as deserving. I want what he sees in me to be true. Maybe I can make it true.

"Okay, I'll find thirty minutes tomorrow to set up my sewing machine on a table in a spot where it can stay out and ready instead of on a shelf in the garage," I announce.

Not with the list of things I have for you when we get home. The Admin tries to squash me.

"Something else may not get done," I voice out loud. I want both Steve and the Admin to hear my decree.

You'll be letting down yourself and your family and your job, argues the Admin.

"I'll be doing something for me, so that's okay if something else doesn't get done," I argue back. Steve is nodding that he likes where this is going.

No, it's not, says the Admin. *Do your work and then you can play. That's the rule.*

"The laundry can wait," I declare. A jolt of freedom courses through me at the mention of putting off the laundry. Deciding what won't get done makes my rebellion all the more real. "I live with a house full of guys. They won't care."

"You're right, they won't care," Steve assures me. "I'm speaking as a guy who has worn the same socks and underwear turned inside out more days than I should."

The laundry has to get done or the boys won't have clean clothes for school. The Admin is seething.

"And your boys will see you do something that makes you happy," Steve adds.

"I hadn't thought of that," I tell him. "You're right."

He's not right, squeaks the Admin. Her voice sounds farther away.

"I'm right about a lot of stuff," boasts Steve. "I don't know if you've noticed, but it's true. It's a good idea to listen to me."

"I'm not sure yet if that's true," I joke. "I'll tell you tomorrow if I think it's a good idea to listen to you or not."

"Trust your instincts, Gail." Steve tries to use an Obi-Wan Kenobi tone with me. It's working. "Especially when I offer to take over driving now so you can rest and get over that migraine. Are you still having the migraine?" he asks me.

"Yes, the band of light is fading, but it's still there," I reply.

"Okay, let's switch." Steve unbuckles himself, then opens his door and gets out of the car.

Gail, you're an idiot, says the Admin from far away, trying to regain authority.

Shut up, I tell her. *I'm trusting my instincts now.* Steve opens the door for me. I get out and walk around the car to the passenger's side. I keep my mind and my mouth silent as we take off again. I close my eyes and try to relax my migraine away. The Admin grumbles in the back, but I don't give her room to speak. Instead, I think about setting up my sewing machine.

120

CHAPTER 17

*N*ellie returns with a tray of beverages. She gives John his coffee, then slides the orange juice past Edgar so he'll move down the bench and let her sit. She's brought a cup of tea for herself and starts to blow on it so it'll cool enough to drink. No one has said anything. Nellie looks over at John, who is clearly agitated and trying to remain calm. As John takes a sip of his coffee, Nellie shoots Edgar a look of confusion and concern. Edgar responds with a small wave of his hand that it'll be okay, but Nellie sees in his eyes that she should get ready for what comes next.

John lowers his coffee cup to see both Edgar and Nellie staring at him. They're waiting for him to start talking. Funny, he was so anxious to start this inquest and now the words seem stuck in his throat. John decides to start with something simple. "I just met Edgar on the airplane," he tells Nellie. "We sat next to each other."

Nellie nods that she's following.

"I'm having trouble forming the words to tell this story," John rubs his thumb over his heart where the harpoon remains lodged. "So I'm going to skip to the end and just say... that my wife left town this morning without telling me. I don't know where she is exactly. I'm trying to follow her so I can find out what's going on. I know that she was here in your restaurant for lunch."

"How do you know she was here?" asks Nellie.

John takes out his phone and shows Nellie the locator dot traveling north. "The blue dot is my wife. Around noon her dot was here. Your restaurant came up as the location."

"Technology today," muses Nellie with awe at what she sees on John's phone. "Next you're going to tell me you have satellite photos of my recipe cards and are putting me out of business. Also, you do know exactly where she is – your wife is right there." Nellie points to Gail's dot. "You can see where she is."

"I can see where she is, yes, but I don't know why she's there or where she's going."

"Why don't you call her?" offers Nellie like the answer is just that easy.

John's shoulders drop as he considers having to give Nellie the story of all that brought him here.

"Let's just let John talk and ask the questions for now," intercedes Edgar. "Okay, sis?"

"Sure, sorry," says Nellie, though John can see she can't understand how her question was that difficult.

"Her name is Gail," John says. He hopes it will ring a bell for Nellie, but he notices that Edgar starts a bit at hearing Gail's name.

"I met a Gail today," Nellie confirms. "Gail and Steve. They're on their way to Vancouver."

The harpoon of fear in John's chest completes its pass through him and exits out his back. Any air that was in his lungs washes out through the hole that is left. John's mind has gone into lockdown, except that it can see one word: Steve. The word Steve is now planted across John's mind like a dam holding back any other thoughts or reasoning.

"Hold on," says Edgar. John tries to shift his focus to Edgar, but the Steve dam in his head makes quick movements impossible. With concentration, John is able to make his eyes travel from Nellie to Edgar. Edgar is looking at John with disbelief. "I didn't ask you your wife's name. Your wife's name is Gail." Edgar then turns to Nellie and asks, "There can't be too many Steve and Gail pairs traveling to Vancouver today, can there? Wait." Edgar pulls out his phone and pulls up a picture of Steve eating a crepe in his restaurant with his daughter, Aria. "Is this the Steve you met?"

"Yes, that's the Steve who was here today," answers Nellie, dumbstruck by this strange turn.

"Why do you have a picture of him on your phone?"

"That's a conversation for later," Edgar says, deflecting his sister. "Gail was here with Steve, and you met them. This shouldn't be the case. They should be in Vancouver by now. Steve was flying them in his plane. Why were they here?"

"Gail and Steve told me they came here in the plane of a friend of mine. I don't know anything about Steve's plane. I guess something happened, and Steve's plane didn't work out," Nellie says slowly, trying to put the pieces together.

As the siblings talk, John's eyes have been focused like lasers on Edgar's phone. At this angle, he can see the outline of a man and a little girl, but he isn't able to focus on any details of the face he wants to see and wishes didn't exist. With profound mental resolve, John extends his arm across the table and holds his hand open in front of Edgar. Edgar looks down at John's hand then looks up to John's face to find John staring at his phone. Gently, Edgar places the phone in John's hand. John doesn't bring his hand any closer to his face. Instead, he maneuvers the phone so the screen is in his direct line of sight. The face of the smiling man burns itself into John's mind. The embers from this branding spit down John's arm to the phone, causing John to drop it on the table like it's a hot coal. John retracts his arm quickly, not wanting to feel the sting of that burn again. Instantly, Edgar scoops his phone off the table and puts it in a pocket so it's out of sight.

John's eyes dart back and forth between Edgar and Nellie. The lockdown on his brain ended when his fear took the form of a smiling face, a solid enemy. John needs answers, but he isn't sure who to question first. He chooses Edgar. "How do you know Gail? How did you know she was going to Vancouver with…" John can't bring himself to say the name.

"Steve," offers Edgar.

"I know his name," John murmurs through clenched teeth. "How do you know them and their plans?"

"They were in my restaurant this morning. Gail had the Strawberry Fields crepe," Edgar begins, searching for a way to explain all he knows to John. "Steve had…"

"I don't care what they ate," says John, whose mind has questions he doesn't want to ask, but must. "Do they eat in your restaurant often?" John can feel the pulse in his temples. The lump in his throat tells him he's about to cry.

John's distress is apparent, so Edgar speaks quickly, "Steve comes in with his daughter every Saturday. Today was my first time to meet Gail. I got the impression Gail and Steve didn't know each other that well. I think Steve took an interest in Gail because he saw he could do something nice for her – give her a day outside her normal life. She looked like she could use it too."

"Why do you say that?" asks John. Edgar's offhanded remark causes the hole in John's chest to flare with fresh pain.

Edgar registers this hurt and knows that he needs to choose his next words carefully. "Gail seemed tightly wound to me. She couldn't relax enough to enjoy breakfast with a nice guy like Steve." John winces at the mention of Steve's name. "It surprised me is all. I would have loved to have breakfast with… him… and Gail was sitting there so stiff and full of nerves. They did not look like a couple on a date. I can promise you that. I think he just wanted to show Gail some fun for a day. They were supposed to get Gail back in time to pick up her kids. I remember that distinctly."

John's mind is reeling. Instead of finding Gail, he's found a sibling duo with unusual answers for him in the booth of a sandwich diner in the Portland airport. How is this his life? And why didn't Gail tell him all this herself?

"Why Vancouver?" John's mind returns to the questioning at hand.

Edgar begins, "It was far enough but close enough for a day—"

Nellie answers at the same time. "There's a fireworks show they're going to see—"

Edgar and John look at Nellie and both say, "What?"

"What fireworks show?" asks Edgar.

"They called it the Celebration of Light fireworks show," answers Nellie. "Only..." Nellie stops as she realizes that she's about to reveal how she's inspired Gail to break federal laws to get to the fireworks show. She's not sure how John will take this.

"Only what?!" asks John, who jerks forward at Nellie like he's about to jump across the table to shake her. Nellie's nerves skyrocket, but she knows she has to tell him. She reaches over and grabs Edgar's hand for support.

"Gail doesn't have her passport," Nellie explains. John nods that he knows this and waves her on to the next point. Nellie turns to Edgar and focuses on him to say what comes next, out of safety. "So I told Gail and Steve about our family property along the border, and how they could cross there undetected."

Edgar's free hand flies up to his mouth out of shock as he utters a muffled, "Oh, Nellie."

"It seemed like the right thing to do," whimpers Nellie, who is now squirming under duress. "They'd come so far, and it seemed important that they make it. It's like they're on a quest, something bigger than a small outing for a day."

Edgar heaves a sigh and says, "I understand," as he pats Nellie's hand.

He's comforting her, thinks John, which causes greater throbbing in his temples as blood rises and pounds above his ears.

"My turn," says Edgar. He looks at John, whose face is red and shaking, and decides to do the same as his sister and direct his confession to her, out of safety. "I told Gail she should go with Steve today. It looked like she wasn't going to do it, which I was happy about at first because I thought maybe I could talk my way into going with him instead."

"Oh, Edgar," says Nellie. "That's why you're here today."

Edgar hangs his head in response, but keeps on with his confession. "I talked Gail into going because I saw how much she needed to break out for a day."

"What is that supposed to mean?!" snaps John. "Break out of what? What was so awful about her life that she had to skip town with..." John's throat closes when he tries to say...

"Steve," offers Edgar, trying to help.

"I know his name," John mutters through clenched teeth, again. Only this time there's a fierce look to go with the statement that makes clear to Edgar that *Steve* is a dangerous word.

Edgar searches for something, anything, to calm John down. "Gail made a point of telling me that she's married." It works. John responds with a look of pure hope for what it could mean. Edgar has thrown him a lifeline. "I was showing her to the ladies' bathroom and we started talking. She was confused over a decision that I would have pounced on. This was not endearing her to me, but then she told me that she's married. She wanted me to know that this trip wasn't about getting time with the model-worthy and talented man sitting at her table who is just as gorgeous on the inside as out, especially when he's with his daughter..."

"Edgar," interrupts Nellie, who wants to keep John in a good mood. Edgar clamps his mouth shut and shoots John a look of apology.

"I'm sorry, John. I've had a crush on... him for quite a while. Gail, however, made clear that she is married and was thinking of you."

"Then why didn't she call me?" John asks.

"I don't know why, John, I'm sorry."

Another wave of anxiety washes through John. This wave is different, though. This wave springs from a well of anger that makes John want to scream and pound something, or someone. Steve. In this instant, John can think on his name and give it powerful focus. Steve took his wife today. That's not the big hurt, though, John realizes. Gail chose to go. She may have told Edgar that she's married and loves her husband, but she chose to go and leave John behind. Edgar may think he talked her into going, but she can make up her own mind. Gail doesn't get talked into anything she doesn't want to do. John knows this much is true about his wife.

This understanding roots John to his seat. All the desire he had to launch himself out of the booth once he figured out what to do next has left him. Gail chose to leave town with another man. For the first time, in his heart and in his marriage, John asks himself why he shouldn't just let her go.

ACT 3

Fireworks

CHAPTER 18

*G*ail looks across a pinewood sawhorse at Steve. The sawhorse is waist high to her. They're standing in someone's front yard. The sun is bright, making the grass and leaves in the yard look yellow, almost golden. There's a party of people standing on the porch and in the yard. Gail sees them talking but doesn't hear anything. The silence doesn't bother Gail, however. To Gail's right is a picnic table of people enjoying food on paper plates. The table has a red gingham tablecloth that almost sparkles in the sunlight.

Steve tells her that there is cheese and wine on the porch. Gail looks over, across the sawhorse, and sees a long table on the porch with an abundant spread of food and drink. The people congregated around the table are laughing, though she still can't hear them. Gail is glad to be at this party. She is ready to go to the porch. She's hungry for cheese and crackers. Steve motions for Gail to follow him. He walks straight up the front steps to the porch. Gail is stunned that he would go that way. She calls out to Steve that he's doing it wrong. The right way is to jump up on the sawhorse and walk along it like a balance beam. Then step over to the picnic table with the red table-cloth and walk across it – avoiding people's food – and launch off the corner of the table to the narrow stone wall that runs along the front of the porch and up the side of the steps. After ascending the stone wall, again like a balance beam, then it's okay to step onto the porch. That's the right way to go.

Steve tells her that's too hard. Gail scoffs and proceeds to show him how it's done. She kicks a foot up onto the sawhorse and steadies herself. Then she brings the other foot up and is able to stand. Gail looks to Steve, who is watching her, and gives him an 'I told you so' look. Then Gail walks to the end of the sawhorse and sees that stepping off of it onto the picnic table is going to be hard. She thinks about how far it is and that she can't just step off onto the bench or she could fall onto the ground. Gail decides to turn herself around on the sawhorse, crouch down, and reach out behind her with a leg so she can get to the picnic table. It works. Gail's foot finds the bench. She shifts her weight so her other foot is on the picnic bench, then Gail pushes off from the sawhorse.

Gail is uncomfortable now, however. This route is harder than she thought it was going to be, and the picnickers are staring at her while guarding their food. Steve steps closer to Gail and offers his hand to help her. She looks at Steve's hand and then looks over at the stone wall. "I don't think I need your help. I think I can jump to the wall on my own."

"Are you sure you don't want to step down and walk up the steps?" asks Steve. Gail realizes that the hand he's offering is to help her off the bench and onto the ground. In that moment, Gail sees that her route may not be the best one after all.

"We're here," Steve says to Gail. The hand he had stretched out to her now gives her a small push, threatening to topple her into people's food. "Gail, we're here," Steve says again. His hand gives another push and then Gail feels herself fall.

* * *

MY FOOT SLAMS down hard on the floor of the passenger side of the car. I wake to my body lifting for a moment, only to be flung back into place by my seat belt. This full body slam back into my seat is as

131

jarring to my nerves as it is to my body. I do a mental scramble to figure out what's happening to me, when I see Steve plastered to the driver's side door with his arms crossed in front of him like he's about to be attacked by some wild animal. I look around and then understand that the wild animal is me. The car is stopped. I get it now. Steve nudged me to wake me from a nap, and I responded by trying to eject myself from my seat. After a few quick breaths, I look over at Steve. He also looks like he's working to calm himself.

"Bad dream?" Steve asks.

"Sorry," I say. "I dreamt I was falling. In fact, I dreamt I was falling because you pushed me."

"Mental note taken – never nudge Gail while she's sleeping," Steve vows with conviction. "I was waking you to let you know we're here."

I look outside the car and see we've stopped in front of a two-story farmhouse that looks worn but inviting. The long porch that wraps around its front has chairs and a porch swing that beckon me to sit a spell and relax. Unlike the sun-kissed porch in my dream, this porch seems to provide a lot of shade. It looks lived on, like the comfortable alternative to a living room on a hot summer night like tonight. I'm so captivated by its charm that I forget for a moment why we're here.

Steve opens his car door to get out. This sound and motion bring me back to reality and glue me to my chair. Steve starts walking toward the house then looks back to see I'm still in the car. He calls out to me, "I'm going to see if anyone is home." Then he continues up to the front door, straight up the steps, just like in my dream. I look around and do not see any other cars parked around the house. I note the lack of a sawhorse in the yard as well.

Steve knocks on the front door and waits a few moments. He knocks again but harder this time to make sure anyone napping in a far bedroom on the second floor can hear him. He waits. No one comes to the door. No one is home. We were hoping this would be the case. The house is a vacation spot for Nellie's family. Nellie called the house to see if anyone would pick up the phone and no one did. Nellie's great aunt Virginia is the official homeowner, she told us, but everyone in the family is free to use it. As luck or providence would have it, today the house is empty.

Steve turns to face me and gives me two thumbs up with a wide grin. He skips off the porch and does a happy jog back to the car. He opens my car door and asks, "Do you want to use the bathroom before we keep going?" I realize that if I stay in the car then our planned criminal act is the next stop on our route. I unbuckle my seat belt and get out of the car. Steve closes the door behind me and then does his happy jog back up to the porch. I approach the house with caution while Steve jogs down the porch and disappears around the side. Though I'm half-frozen with what we're about to do, I cannot help but be struck by how happy this house makes me. *If I had access to a place like this I would be here every weekend,* I think. *Except that I wouldn't. I would want to be here, but there would be too much to do to make it happen. Maybe those in Nellie's family feel the same way. Maybe having a house like this as an option on your weekend just makes the toil at home harder. God, I can be a downer.*

No argument here, says the Admin.

Steve jogs back from around the house with a key in his hand. "It was right where Nellie said it would be," he tells me. Steve goes to the front door, unlocks it, and pushes it open. He extends his arm over the threshold as an invitation to enter. I take a breath and walk inside, again with caution. It's weird to enter someone else's house when they're not home.

The inside of the house is even more charming than the outside. The walls display art done by children, someone's decoupage of leaves with sheets of poetry, and several framed family photos. The furniture and floors look well-used and well-loved. I venture into a sitting room that is right inside the front door and see a large fireplace with a mantel lined with homemade trophies. I can't help but take a closer look at the hand-crafted pieces made of toilet rolls, spray-painted action figures, offcuts of wood, and anything else you'd find in a crafts bin. Each of the trophies has a laminated placard at its base announcing the award title. I read the placards and see that awards have been given for Best Spam Pie Maker and Fastest Runner (Away from a Snake). There's a trophy for Most Unusual Lunch that has a figure made of popsicle stick pieces chasing a ceramic skunk. Next to the skunk trophy is one that reads Best-Dressed DJ. Above this placard stands a Ken doll dressed in a pink wig, a pink tutu, and black boots. Black leather shoelaces cross his bare chest. A dollhouse record player stands at Ken's feet. Curiouser and curiouser, I think, feeling amused and dumbfounded by the entire display.

I glance over and see Steve is studying a picture of two kids. I walk over to see what he finds so interesting. Steve sees me coming and says, "Take a look at this one. I think the girl is probably Nellie. She looks about twelve. What's strange is that the boy standing next to her looks familiar to me. Does he remind you of anyone?"

I look at the young boy and can't see anything about him that I recognize. "Sorry, no."

"Huh," says Steve. "Well, let's find the toilet and be on our way." Steve walks to the other side of the room and through a door. After a few seconds I hear him call out, "Found it! Do you want to go first?"

"No, go ahead," I reply. I try to read some of the poetry in a decoupage piece on the wall when I hear a noise from the other side of the house. The noise is a screen door opening then slamming shut. I freeze where I stand, hardly able to breathe. Has someone broken in? Yes, we have. No, we were invited. We came in with a key. Is this person part of the family? I should go to Steve. No, I should call out to the person. No, keep your mouth shut. What should I do? Great, the Admin isn't answering. Just when I need to be told what to do, she goes into hiding.

I hear footsteps. The other person is walking toward me. I should say something. I should announce myself. The other person goes first. From a couple of rooms away, a young man's voice sings out, "Scooby Dooby Do, where are you? We got some work to do now." It's the Scooby Doo theme song. The man sung it out like he expected a reply. I wish I knew the words, but I don't.

"Um, hi," I say in a kind of sing-songy voice, then think better of that and stop. In my regular voice I say, "Hi, hello, I'm in the living room." The footsteps stop for a second at the sound of my voice – a voice this person doesn't recognize – then they start again and continue approaching. A moment later, he appears in the doorway with a quizzical look on his face. I nearly bust out with one of my laughs when I see him, partly because my nerves are frayed, but mainly because his hair is pink. His hair is as pink as pink could ever hope to be pink. The pink hair stands up in short spikes all over his head, which, coupled with the quizzical look, makes him look like a lean and modern Troll doll. I manage to stifle the bomb of giggles set to blow. Instead, I put my hand out to shake his and introduce myself.

"Hi, I'm Gail." Mr. Pink shakes my hand then takes a cautious step back from me. "I'm here with my friend, Steve, who is using the bathroom right now. Nellie…" I pause at Nellie's name when I realize that for the second time today I'm following the lead of a person whose last name I don't know. "Nellie in Portland said we could come to her family house, which is lovely by the way. She told us where to find the hidden key. We came in with a key." I repeat the part about the key to ensure he knows we didn't break in.

"Okay," he says. "You met Nellie in her diner?"

"Yes, we both had the egg salad sandwich. It was the best sandwich I think I've ever had."

This seems to confirm for the young man that we do really know Nellie, and he relaxes a bit. "I'm Peep," he tells me.

"Excuse me?"

"My name is Peep, like the marshmallow treat at Easter."

"Okay," is all I can think to say. With luck, Steve enters the room at that moment. I turn to him in time to see the utter surprise on his face that is followed by a subtle grin that I know is a stifled laugh, same as mine. "Here's my friend, Steve. Steve, this is Peep."

"Excuse me?" says Steve.

"P-E-E-P," explains Peep. "My name is Peep. How long are you guys staying?"

Steve and I look at each other. We're both unsure what we should reveal to a guy whose name comes from a sticky Easter treat. "We're just passing through," says Steve. "Nellie told us about this place and its history. She invited us to stop here and take a look at the tunnel the rum runners used."

"None of us talk about the tunnel. It's a closely guarded family secret." Peep is now eyeing us. "Nellie must have told you about it so you can use it, to get into Canada."

Steve and I stare at Peep. Peep looks at me, then at Steve, then back at me. He takes a breath while he thinks over why we're here then tells us, "It doesn't matter to me. Use the tunnel. If you're caught and expose the tunnel, then I never saw you. I'm not even supposed to be here today."

"Nellie gave us some directions on how to find the tunnel, but do you have a couple of minutes to show us where it is?" This is shrewd of Steve to ask, but it makes my nerves jump.

Peep sighs and thinks it over while he checks us both out again. A part of me hopes we're cool enough for Peep. Another hopes he tells us off for trying to make him an accomplice. Then another part of me remembers that "I need to use the bathroom first, please."

Steve nods at me, then looks at Peep with raised eyebrows indicating he's still waiting on an answer to his question.

Peep shrugs and says, "Sure, I'll point it out to you." Peep looks over at me. "Go use the can. I'll wait."

I nod my thanks and do a quick shuffle out of the room. I skip down a short hallway, aware all of a sudden that I do really need to use the toilet. I find the bathroom at the end of the hall. Once I'm seated in the bathroom with the door closed, I realize I could stall in here.

You can't stay here forever, remarks the Admin. *Just tell Steve you're not doing this. It's illegal. The respectable thing to do is stop now.*

I don't want to go to jail, I think.

Exactly, agrees the Admin.

I need to think of my family, I reason.

Calling home from jail doesn't set a good example for the kids, speaks the Admin from her soap box. Of course, she's right. I can't go forward. I work on the words I'll say to Steve. He won't understand. He'll argue and try to talk me into going, especially after all we've done to get this far. I'll say that I know we've come a long way, but now we're going to do something serious that will get us into a lot of trouble that we don't want. I can hear my Mom voice piping up with the "it's-time-to-be-reasonable" tone. The Admin is close to doing backflips of joy over this turn I've taken. It feels right. It's a relief. I'll be going home.

I finish on the toilet and move to the sink. While washing my hands, I look myself over in the mirror above the sink. I do the regular check of my makeup and hair and see that there's a great deal about me that looks out of place. I can't believe I'm as disheveled as I look. I try running my fingers through my hair in an attempt to look composed before facing Steve. Then it happens. Something new, something different, pops out at me from my eyes. What is that? My eyes are different. Is something wrong with me? I stare into them, trying to figure out what's going on. I move my face closer to the mirror to look deep into my own eyes. I'm a millimeter away from being nose to nose with myself when a flash of understanding hits me like lightning. I can see me in my eyes. I'm not just looking at me. I'm seeing me. For a second I'm tempted to look away, but I don't. The difference is startling, but it's good. Not different, though, because I can remember I used to look this way. Memories flood from some hidden dam of when I used to look this way. In those memories, I liked me. Now I see me again in this mirror.

"Gail, are you ready?" asks Steve from the other side of the bathroom door. "I don't know if Peep will wait much longer."

How odd, I think to myself, still gazing deep into my own eyes. I like who I see in the mirror. It's been a while. "Nice to see you, Gail," I tell the kind and confident woman who's smiling back at me.

"Gail?" Steve says with a small knock on the door.

"I'm ready."

CHAPTER 19

*W*e rejoin Peep in the front room. "We're ready to go, Peep. Thanks for helping us find the tunnel," says Steve. Peep shrugs and turns to walk through the front door. As we both start walking to follow Peep out the door, Steve catches me grinning to myself. My partner in crime does a double-take that almost makes him trip through the door.

"Are you okay?" I ask Steve.

"I'm good, thanks. How are you?"

"I'm good," I tell him with a grin.

"I can see that. It's a little surprising. You're never in a good mood after you get some time alone. I was kind of expecting you to come out of the bathroom and tell me you're not going through the tunnel and want to go home," quips Steve.

"It's not fair that you know me this well after just a few hours."

"Were you going to try and stop here?"

"I thought about it."

"What changed your mind?"

"I did. I changed my mind. I looked in the mirror, and the woman staring back at me looked confident. I like her, so I reconsidered going home. I think I can figure out what to do if we get caught. If I stop now, however, I'm not sure the woman I just saw in the mirror will still be there when I get home." Putting words to my bathroom experience like this seems to explain it all to me as well as to Steve. Expressing myself aloud is something I'm going to do more.

A light bulb goes on over my head. "Peep! Are you the best-dressed DJ from the trophy?"

"Yeah, that's me." Peep grins.

"Is the pink tutu with leather straps your regular DJ outfit?" I ask, feeling slightly naughty.

"No," replies Peep who stops next to our car. "We had a fancy-dress dinner where neighbors were invited. I offered to DJ the party, and my Great Aunt Victoria said okay. She doesn't even know the kind of music I play. I showed up early to set up. I was wearing the outfit you saw on the trophy, with my hair dyed pink for the first time. I just wanted a reaction. Aunt Victoria looked me over, and I remember being disappointed because she didn't look that surprised. Her eyes focused on my hair and stayed there. She stared at my hair for what seemed like forever. I was waiting for some comment on the outfit and for her to tell me that I need to go change my clothes. Instead, she said, "Your hair looks like the Peep marshmallow treats at Easter. Peeps are my favorite." That's it. She didn't say anything about the tutu or the leather straps. She didn't ask me to change."

"Did anyone else say anything at the party?" Steve asks.

"No," says Peep. "I decided to put on a suit I had brought as a backup and let my pink hair make my statement. That night I also started telling everyone to call me Peep. A couple of days later, the trophy was on the mantel. Aunt Victoria made it, of course. My mom asked Aunt Victoria why she dressed the doll like that. Aunt Victoria said, "Peep may have a worn a suit to the party, but in his heart he was wearing a tutu and leather. I actually think she was disappointed that I changed clothes."

"I think I'd like to meet your Aunt Victoria," I say.

Peep smiles and nods his head. "Get in your car and wait here. I'll be right back." With that, Peep turns and jogs to the free-standing garage a few feet away. Steve and I get in the car. We wait for just a couple of minutes before we hear the roar of a motorcycle engine from the garage. Steve takes that as his cue and starts our car. A moment later, Peep emerges on a bright yellow Ducati wearing a matching bright yellow helmet. It's the same yellow as the chick marshmallow treats you can get alongside the peeps at Easter.

Peep looks over at us to see if we're ready. Steve waves back at him. My heart does a sort of flutter. My hands clasp each other in my lap as I lean forward to bounce in my seat. I'm excited to see the tunnel. I want to know what happens next.

Ten minutes later, we're deep into the property, surrounded by trees and hills. We pass a pond that is perfectly still. Its absolute calm holds my full attention for as long as I'm able to see it. I feel a pang of jealousy for the pond that can be so calm. The pond's job is to be calm. It waits for whomever may happen by. Its place of business is this wooded area. The pond gets to work from home. Before I dive too deeply into the health and medical benefits of the pond, I notice Steve is approaching a ridge where Peep has parked his motorcycle. The ridge is lined with trees along its top edge. If we had met this part of the ridge and continued down it, then I don't think I would have given the trees a second look. Now that we're parked close to our destination, I see that the trees line up a little too straight for nature to have done this herself. They are the key to finding the tunnel.

We get out of the car and join Peep, who is waiting for us at the base of the ridge. It's only when we get a few feet away from Peep that I can distinguish from the rest of nature a large handmade curtain of hanging moss, bramble, and thin roots. The curtain extends down from the trees above. As we step closer to the curtain and Peep, I see the sheet of camouflage mesh that is the lining support of this living cover.

"This tunnel is hidden better now than when it was used. All the natural growth has helped to cover it convincingly," says Peep as he unzips his motorcycle jacket halfway down his torso and reaches inside it. Peep produces two pairs of work gloves and distributes them to Steve and me. "You won't need your gloves now," Peep says to me, "but you will need them on the other side." With that, Peep stoops down and shuffles aside leaves that have fallen from the sentry line of trees. We see him uncover a beam of wood that holds the bottom border of the curtain in place.

"Grab the other end of this beam," Peep says to Steve. Steve follows the beam down a few feet until he locates the end. He wraps his hands around the end and waits for Peep to show him what comes next. Peep starts to lift the beam and Steve follows suit. When they have the beam a few inches off the ground, I see that it's around three inches think. It's substantial, but I believe I can handle its brother on the other end of the tunnel as long as they're twins. Peep and Steve lift the beam over their heads. Peep then moves the beam close to the ridge and places it in a bracket I would never have seen if Peep hadn't used it. The bracket looks like an outgrowth of wood and moss from the side of the ridge except that it forms a perfect 'U' for the beam to rest inside. Steve finds his bracket on the other end.

The three of us take a moment to stare into the black abyss that has appeared. It frightens me how big it looks now that we've uncovered the tunnel. It could swallow us up, and no one would ever find us. Peep starts to giggle, which catches me off-guard. Steve and I both snap our heads to look at him and see what's so funny. We could use a joke about now.

"You should see how terrified you both look," Peep says in between chuckles. "If you think this tunnel looks scary now, just wait a sec." With that, Peep walks two feet into the tunnel and pulls a blanket off a very old-looking machine with a crank handle. I notice there are wires coming out of it that run up the wall of the tunnel to the top edge of the wall and then turn into the tunnel and disappear. Peep turns the crank about a dozen times or more, then flips a toggle switch on the side of the box. Lights turn on about every twenty feet down the tunnel. This is impressive. I'm relieved that I can see the inside of the tunnel, until I realize how much scarier it looks now that I can see it. There are roots covered in moss and spider webs growing through the ceiling, and something that I don't want to think about slithered away when the lights came on. I don't like what I see, but it occurs to me that it would be a lot worse traversing this tunnel in the dark.

Peep reaches behind the generator and pulls out something long that's wrapped in a thin blanket. He unwraps the blanket to reveal a large machete that looks well-used and as dangerous as a machete can look when you're not the person holding it. Every Stephen King novel I've ever read – and I've read a few – flashes before me. I'm sure that we're about to be killed by a pink-haired DJ named Peep. Our bodies will be deposited in this tunnel that will now do just as I thought it could and swallow us whole, hiding our remains forever.

Instead, Peep hands the machete to Steve. "You're going to need to clear away the hanging roots so your car doesn't get scratched. Gail can drive with the headlights on behind you as you clear. The tunnel is about a half-mile long. You're going to get a workout." Steve gives the machete a long look. He's not happy about his job but looks resigned nonetheless. "Be careful you don't hurt the wiring," continues Peep. "We've never replaced anything. This lighting rig is older than Great Aunt Victoria."

Steve nods that he understands, then turns to me. "Time to get ourselves down the rabbit hole."

CHAPTER 20

*W*e both thank Peep over and over for helping us get here. Finding the tunnel, raising the curtain, and turning on the lights would not have gone so well without him. Plus, we never would have known about the machete. Steve and Peep shake hands while Steve thanks him for the fifth or sixth time. I stick my hand out to shake Peep's hand too. Peep looks down at my hand and studies it for a second. Then he opens his arms wide as an invitation. I can't pass up a hug from Peep. I walk into his arms to say good-bye. As he hugs me, Peep leans his head down so his mouth is close to my ear and says, "Whatever clicked for you in the bathroom has done wonders for you. Your face has opened up. You look happy." Peep releases me, and I look up into his face. I'm stunned that my brief encounter of self was that apparent or transformative. Peep smiles at my dismay and says, "I know what that kind of click feels like. It happened for me when Aunt Victoria gave me my name."

Peep takes a few steps backward, holding his smile for me. Then he turns and walks to his bike. As he starts his motorcycle and puts on his helmet, I stand still and watch him with wonder and gratitude. Peep can see me. I saw me in the mirror. Now Peep sees me too and he understands. How important and magnificent it is to feel someone can see me. Tears spring to my eyes as Peep gets on his bike. He kicks back his kickstand and gives us a last wave before walking his bike around in a tight circle to point himself in the right direction and take off.

I wipe the tears from my face. The sight of me in the mirror springs to the forefront of my mind. I want to hold onto that vision of me. I walk over to the car, thinking about grabbing a peek at me in the visor mirror, when I look over at Steve, who has taken off his shirt. His bare chest surprises me. Not only because I didn't expect the nakedness, but also because he is beautiful with his shirt off. I wonder for a moment why he would ever put a shirt on if this is how he looks without it. Steve sees my surprise and is embarrassed by it. He moves to cross his arms to hide himself, but the machete in one hand gets in the way. Instead, he manages one arm crossed over his chest while the other drops to the side, keeping a firm grip on the machete. If we were in a strip club, he'd be playing the part of the sexy yet shy jungle explorer. I can also imagine him on the cover of a romance novel.

"I... took off... I took my shirt off." Steve is stammering. I love this. "I took my shirt off so it doesn't get dirty. I don't have another one."

"Sure, that makes sense. Good thinking," I say to him, doing my best not to stare at him too long. He drops his arm from his chest and starts walking toward me. The unannounced, sudden movement catches me off-guard. I don't know what he's about to do but the rush of blood charging up my face lets me know I'm excited. Steve walks straight to me then straight past me and to the car. He opens the car door and throws his shirt inside. Steve takes a step back from the car with the door open and extends his arm toward the driver's seat as a signal that I should get in.

"Let's get going," Steve says. He's still embarrassed.

"You shouldn't be so embarrassed. You look... good." Now I'm stammering. I can see I'm not helping.

"Thanks, let's just get moving, okay?" Steve is no longer able to look at me, and I now feel as embarrassed as he looks about my stunted compliment. I avert my eyes and get into the driver's seat of the car. Steve closes the door after me and marches into the tunnel.

I start the engine and put the car in gear. I can already hear hacking sounds coming from the tunnel. I press on the gas pedal with the smallest pressure possible so I creep over to the tunnel. I do my best to position the car so it points straight into the center of the opening. The tunnel is big enough for the car to get through on either side, but not by much. What impresses me is how tall the tunnel is – maybe as tall as eight or nine feet. I see Steve stretch up to clear the lower-hanging roots so the car can pass through. My mind noodles on the tunnel height as an attempt to keep from imagining Steve's gorgeous, moist-from-sweat torso against me in a variety of positions. Then I think I figure it out. The rum runners were probably driving trucks. The trucks would be tall and laden with as many barrels or boxes of rum as the trucks could hold.

I want to tell Steve how clever I am about figuring out why the tunnel is tall. I start to roll the window down to call out to him, but I decide it's not a good idea to distract him now while he's at work wielding a large knife. I close the window. My clever comment can wait. I need something new to think about.

Something new appears on cue. A snake drops on the hood of the car from the roof of the tunnel. I'm stunned. I stare at the snake, who stares back at me. My foot comes off the gas pedal. The car rolls to a slow stop. I'm not moving, the car isn't moving, and the snake isn't moving. The snake must be as stunned as I am. Then the snake moves. The snake moves fast. The snake launches itself from the hood toward the wall of the tunnel. I scream and punch the horn of the car. Steve jumps and flips himself around to see what's going on. The arm holding the machete swings in front of him, following a long arc that curves wide above his shoulder and ends in the top corner of the tunnel wall. The blade of the machete hits the wires that carry electricity to the bulbs that light our way. Sparks fly when this connection is made, and we are plunged into darkness. I panic.

"Steve!" I call out to him. I see Steve standing still, looking amazed at what he's just done. His hand leaves the machete that is still stuck inside the wall where it made contact. My brain acknowledges that I can see Steve, so we haven't plunged into full darkness after all. The car headlights have prevented that. Both Steve and I meet each other's eyes. Mine are still full of panic. I watch as Steve's eyes turn from chagrin to anger as he looks at me. I can see that he's going to demand some answers about what just happened, but he doesn't get the chance. A flame bursts from where the machete rests in the wall. The sparks we saw must have landed on dry roots or bramble. Steve grabs the machete handle and pulls on it, but the machete stays put. The flame spreads to the surrounding tendrils of wood and moss. A dangerous fire starts inside 2.3 seconds. The fire is above us on the ceiling of the tunnel and is spreading both forward and behind us.

Steve looks to the sides of the car and sees he can't get in and I can't get out. The doors are too close to the walls. He looks at me and shouts, "Come on!" Then Steve turns and runs. Steve is leaving. I should leave too.

My brain works enough for me to put my foot down on the gas pedal and get the car moving. I catch up to Steve. My feet work the gas and brake pedals to keep up with Steve but not run him over. My eyes stayed glued to Steve while the surrounding tunnel walls and roof spring to a fiery life of orange and white and red. The roof of the car crashes through fire-licked hanging tendrils of roots that shower the windshield and obstruct my view of Steve. Out of instinct, I turn on the windshield wipers. They don't help.

I think I see the end of the tunnel. There's a curtain over it at the entrance, but there's light peeking through. In my periphery, I see the fire racing alongside the car and I wonder which of us will reach the end of the tunnel first.

Steve's arms and legs are pumping hard to keep him ahead of the car and get him out as fast as they can. We're near the end. The light through the curtain is stronger and closer. I see what looks like stacked boulders around the edge of the entrance. My headlights catch a flicker off a steel band, and my mind registers that the boulders are barrels. There are barrels on either side of the exit posted like sentries standing single file against both walls. Some are stacked three barrels high. I don't know if the car will fit between them. What if they're full of something?

As though intense fear can induce a psychic link, Steve screams an answer to me over his shoulder, "Drive through the barrels! Just get out!" My foot responds by pressing harder on the gas in case I need momentum to get through the barrels. Steve's already frantic pace steps up to keep him ahead of me.

Steve sprints to the end of the tunnel and slides out the side of the curtain before I can blink. For one second, I'm alone in the tunnel. My fear spikes. The car's front bumper starts crashing through barrels. I feel the car labor to get through them but my speed doesn't falter. I see splashes of liquid cross the windshield that look brown and muddy. Oh God, is it gas?

Before God can answer, the car delivers me through the curtain and outside the tunnel. The curtain covers my windshield. I can't see ahead of me. I turn the steering wheel hard to the right while I stand on the brake pedal with both feet. Through the driver's side window I see that I'm careening sideways toward a line of trees. The car stops, however, before it hits the tree line. The car has stopped. The windshield wipers are removing enough of the curtain so I can see Steve running around the front of the car to the driver's side. I want him to run faster.

A flash of light and a sound like exploding dynamite comes from the tunnel. I feel a wave of air rush through the car. I press myself against the door, scared of what may fly at me. I hear things smash against the passenger side. Something hits the window and cracks it. I scream. My arms cover my head in case the next thing to hit the cracked window flies through it. I wait, but there is nothing. I hear crackling and a dull roar that is the tunnel fire. Next, I hear the handle of my car door being tugged several times in rapid succession. It startles my already frayed nerves and causes me to jump a few inches out of my seat and scream again.

"Gail! Are you okay? Unlock the door!" Steve is shouting at me. I look through the window at him. Steve looks terrified. "Unlock the door, Gail!" Steve shouts this at me again and points to the lock button to help me understand. I press the button and hear the door lock release. Steve swings the door open and crouches next to me. He puts his hands on my upper arms to turn me toward him. I see him looking over my face and body for damage. I follow his eyes to look for myself. I don't see blood. I think I'm okay. I look back into Steve's face. I can't talk yet, so my eyes ask him if it's okay to cry.

Steve pulls me out of the car and into his arms. My face plants itself in his chest. A sobbing cry springs from me with a force that makes breathing difficult. I gasp for air as best I can as each sob is ejected from my lungs up through my mouth. Steve holds onto me but also starts moving us away from the car. The fire is raging. Flames lick the tunnel entrance. We stand wrapped in each other. Steve watches the fire as I cry out the terror of the past few minutes.

I turn my head toward the heat of the fire out of fear we may be standing too close to it. As hot as it feels, the fire is a safe distance away inside the tunnel. My breathing makes it too hard to speak still, so I gesture to the field of wood fragments strewn between the tunnel and the car.

"The barrels," says Steve. I remember the liquid on the windshield. I keep my arms around Steve's waist while I move us both over to the windshield. My hand reaches out and swipes drops of liquid onto my fingers. I bring my fingers to my nose. The smell is acrid, but it doesn't smell like gasoline. I hold my fingers up to Steve's nose. Steve sniffs at my fingers. Then he grabs my hand with one of his and brings my fingers up against his nose for a good whiff. A second later he puts his mouth over my fingertips to taste the liquid.

"I think it's rum," he tells me. "Very old, awful rum." Steve turns his head away from me as he tries to spit the taste out of his mouth.

Meanwhile, the sensation I felt when his mouth covered my fingertips is spreading up my arm like a spark from the fire. My chest feels warm. I examine my fingertips to see if they've turned red to match the heat I feel radiating from them now.

"I'm sorry, Gail," says Steve. Why is he sorry? For licking my fingers? I feel myself turning red. I shouldn't have enjoyed that.

No, you shouldn't have, scolds the Admin.

"I'm sorry for this mess we're in," explains Steve.

He's sorry for the fire. Is he serious? "I honked the horn at a snake. There was a snake," I say through quivering teeth and lips. "I scared you and made you drive the machete into the tunnel wall. It's my fault. I'm so sorry." I dissolve back into the sobbing tears. Steve holds me close and tells me it isn't my fault. His comfort feels good; so does his chest.

Shame on you, admonishes the Admin again.

I know. This feels good, though. As I think this, I can feel the Admin's temperature rise. She's about to blow.

It reminds me of how I used to feel with John.

Used to? asks the Admin.

I know how bad that sounds. I want to feel this again. I try to think of John. It seems like the right thing to do – to have my husband in mind while a half-naked hunk has his arms around me. The warmth of Steve's holding me makes it difficult to hold John in my mind. A question is inside my head, though. It nags at me. Can I still feel like this with John? I don't want to go there. I want to enjoy this time with Steve.

How great that you have Steve to make you feel so good, goads the Admin.

It is great, actually. Bad, I know, but great just the same.

You're a whore, declares the Admin. The Admin is right. If I stay in his arms, then something will happen. I want it to happen. I turn my face and body into Steve. My hands are on his back. I press into him for a moment. My lips are against his skin, so I can almost taste him. I take in a quick breath, allowing the smell of him to enter me, and then I let go of Steve and take a step back.

"What do we do now?" I ask him, still trembling.

Steve looks at the tunnel. "The fire is pretty big and can spread outside the tunnel. Who knows what's happening on the other end. The explosion was loud, but I don't know if there was anyone else close enough to hear it."

"We need to call for help." I half state this and half pose it as a question to Steve.

"Yes, we need to get firefighters out here."

"We're going to get caught," I tell him.

"I guess so."

Our adventure has ended.

CHAPTER 21

*J*ohn was not expecting an adventure today. Not that his heart is in it. His heart was torn from him an hour ago when he learned his wife was with another man. Still, John can't ignore the intoxication – part fear and part thrill – that comes with sitting in Lucy as she zooms over beautiful countryside. He feels sorry for Gail, knowing that she was on the floor during her trip. Scratch that. John decides that he doesn't feel sorry for Gail, and that he hopes she was nauseous the whole time. John is grappling with wanting to find Gail and hold her close and tight to him, versus wanting to yell mean, horrible things at her. He wonders if he could do both, hold her while he yells at her.

The chasm in John's chest is edged with flaps of skin and soul that slap at his ribs. John notices himself rubbing at his chest, trying to ease the sharp pain away. What will happen when he sees Gail? John has no idea. He wants to believe that she'll be glad to see him, that she'll be impressed with how he followed her and found her. He wants to believe this because then he knows he can yell at her. If she isn't glad to see him, if she was distancing herself from him emotionally as well as physically today, then his world will crumble and him with it.

Then there's Steve, but John can't go there yet.

Lucy makes her descent into New Hope. John looks around and sees the open field behind Ned's house. The ground comes up quickly, making John lift his feet from Lucy's floor out of fear that they may drag or be called upon to slow the craft in true Fred Flintstone fashion. Instead, Ned lands Lucy like she's a feather alighting herself on Mother Earth. John is grateful and, even though he doesn't believe in a man with a beard in the sky watching over him, he still mutters a small thank you prayer under his breath.

"You can unlatch the back doors and step out," Ned instructs John, who does just that. With one step, John leaves his seat and the aircraft at the same time.

"Hello, hello!" Coming toward them, John sees a woman wearing a sequined fireworks sweater and a large grin on her face. She's elated. She extends her hand out to greet him.

"Hello, John. I'm Sheriff Tracy Burnham. I'm so glad to meet you."

"Thank you, Sheriff, and thank you for letting me tag along with you today," says John as he takes her hand.

Sheriff Tracy places her other hand over his and gives him a little tug toward her while looking straight into his eyes as she says, "It's kismet, John. I believe in this stuff. You're meant to be here or you wouldn't have met Ned at Nellie's. Gail was meant to be here or she wouldn't have swung on a trapeze with me today. It did her wonders. I'd get you on that trapeze too if we had the time."

"Gail swung on a trapeze today?" John asks with disbelief. Sheriff Tracy winks at John and gives him a knowing grin before releasing his hand. John has no idea how to respond to that.

"We get to take a whole other ride of a lifetime while we connect you with Gail in Vancouver. This is almost too fun to be legal!"

John acknowledges Sheriff Burnham's joke with a bob of his head and half a grin.

"Oh, buck up, John. I don't think things are near as bad as you're fearing they are. Hey there, Ned!" Sheriff Tracy calls past John to Ned.

"Sheriff," Ned responds.

"You've had quite the day for passengers, haven't you?" asks Sheriff Tracy with a giggle.

"Yes, ma'am," says Ned.

"Why look at how you're glowing, Ned! I've never seen you sparked up like this. Excited for what you get to pilot today? Or are you excited about seeing Nellie again so soon?"

John sees that Ned is taken off-guard by this comment. He thinks Ned may even be blushing.

"I need to grab some stuff. John, do you want to use the... john?" asks Ned.

"I'm fine for now," replies John as he watches Ned duck into his house, so quickly that he is inside with the front door closed behind him before John says, "Thanks, Ned."

"Well, what is that about, do you suppose?" Sheriff Tracy asks out loud, studying Ned's front door. John doesn't think the question is aimed at him, so he doesn't hazard a guess. "You, I can read like a book, however." Sheriff Tracy turns her full attention back to him. She's looking straight into him again. "You're scared because Gail is out there with a guy you don't know. He's nice to look at too. You should know that before you meet him."

"Okay. Thanks. I guess." John cannot figure out how to have a conversation with Sheriff Burnham.

"Loosen up, John, I'm trying to help you. What Gail is out doing today is getting back in touch with Gail. She told me she'd lost sight of herself, and I could see that she was right."

"Why couldn't she tell me that?" asks John. Sheriff Tracy considers John's question, while continuing to stare into his eyes. Her stare is both disconcerting and captivating. If she can read him like a book, then maybe she can find answers in his eyes, or somewhere behind them as her stare bores its way through his skull.

"I don't really know what's keeping Gail from calling you and telling you where she is and what she's doing. I can't answer for Gail. What I'm sitting here wondering is why you're doing the same thing. Your wife doesn't know where you are, who you're with, or what you're doing. Why don't you call her?"

"I tried to call her as my plane was leaving Portland, and I didn't get through," answers John.

"That was your last attempt?" inquires the sheriff. John tries to think of what to say next but is saved by Ned coming out of his house.

"Ready," says Ned, who doesn't stop but walks past them to his truck. "You want to follow me, Sheriff?"

"Sounds good," says Sheriff Tracy. "Would you like to ride with me, John?"

"No, thanks, Sheriff Burnham. I think I'll ride with Ned." John is ready for a break from the sheriff's kismet talk.

"Suit yourself," she replies, "but you're not escaping me for long. We're taking that ride to Vancouver together, you know." Sheriff Tracy gives John another wide smile before getting into her car and starting it up. John gives the sheriff a small wave in return and climbs into Ned's truck. As John puts his seatbelt on, he glances over to Ned, who glances back to John. Neither says a word. Instead, they give each other a knowing nod of gratitude for the silence they'll both enjoy during this leg of their journey.

CHAPTER 22

*T*here is smoke coming from the charred remains of the tunnel. The firefighters arrived before we had the chance to make a call for help, and now they have put the fire out. From the moment they showed up, Steve has had me in his arms comforting me, and himself I think. My mind is splintered – enjoying the embrace, fearing the legal consequences to come, and wondering if I should say something to Steve about my attraction to him – and I can't seem to focus.

One of the firefighters emerges from the tunnel. Fear of jail wins out, and I drop my arms from Steve to bring them across my chest. The anxiety of what happens next grips me like a clamp across my ribs. The firefighter is in full fire protection gear with a helmet covering his face and neck. Even though this person just came out of a dark place of smoke and ash, the suit is a gleaming silver. It reminds me of the old movies about aliens from other planets, which increases my fear of what's lurking below the suit.

The firefighter has the machete in his hand. He looks around, then sees me and Steve standing on the far side of our destroyed car. He walks over to us. The firefighter tucks his free hand under his opposite arm to remove his glove. Something is strange about the hand.

The hand is small, and the fingernails are painted. The hand reaches up and removes the helmet, revealing that the firefighter is a woman. I think Steve had the same incorrect idea concerning the gender of this firefighter that I did. He looks as caught off guard as I feel. She's tall, so the mistake was easy to make. However, that is where the comparisons to a man end. She is beyond beautiful. My anxiety shifts. It occurs to me that Steve is not only caught off guard by her gender, but also by her good looks. I don't like this.

You're married. How many times do I have to tell you this today? states the Admin. *So what if Steve is attracted to her?*

I know I shouldn't be jealous, I tell the Admin, *but I am. I've been through a lot with John today, and I'm not ready to lose his attention.*

Did you just say John? asks the Admin.

Did I? I wonder.

"Hello," the lady firefighter says as her eyes move to acknowledge both Steve and me. "How are you holding up?" Her eyes are on me now. I try to think of an answer, but all I can process is how green her eyes are and how they seem to sparkle in the sun. Damn her green eyes.

"I think we're okay," says Steve. The emerald orbs shift to look at him. I look up at Steve as well and see that he's transfixed by her. Of course he is.

The lady firefighter nods in response then looks down at the machete she's holding. "Can one of you tell me what happened?" she asks.

"The machete hit the wiring for the lights along the tunnel and sparked a fire. It's my fault," admits Steve.

"It's my fault," I pipe up. "A snake dropped on the hood of the car, and I honked the horn at it, which scared Steve. Steve was using the machete to clear branches out of the way of the car, and the horn made his arm fly." I illustrate the arm movement to the beautiful firefighter so she understands, then I feel stupid for doing that and drop my arm.

"The car horn shocked me," Steve tries to explain to the lady firefighter. "I wasn't scared." Great, he's trying to impress her.

"Anyway," I continue, "the... shock... of the car horn caused Steve's arm to swing around and plant the machete in the tunnel wall. It was an accident."

The lady firefighter turns to Steve for confirmation. He obliges. "She's right. I didn't mean to cut the wire. It was an accident."

"Okay," says the lady firefighter. "We've stopped the fire. Thankfully, it didn't leave the tunnel. All the brush and trees around here are dried out this time of year. It's high fire season."

"Is that why you responded so fast?" asks Steve. "You're watching for fires? Did you see the smoke?"

"Peep called me," she tells us. She sees our surprise at the mention of Peep's name. "Peep and I have played in this tunnel our whole lives. Peep saw the smoke and called me. He knows I volunteer with the fire brigade over here. He called the local brigade on his end too."

"You've known Peep since you were a kid?" asks Steve, prying for information on the lady firefighter and just wanting to keep the conversation going, I suspect.

"That's right," she answers.

"So you know his real name?" asks Steve.

"His real name is Peep," she tells Steve with a set look in her eye.

"Right, that's right, of course, sorry," Steve stammers, trying to recover. "I guess I was really wondering what your name is." Steve looks sheepish that he may have blown this, which makes him look irresistible as well. Damn his irresistible sheepishness.

You're wrong to be bothered, chides the Admin.

You're right that I'm wrong, I tell her to get her to go away again.

Grow up and drop this. You're married, you idiot, and Steve wouldn't go for you anyway, she tells me.

I like his attention, I confess. *I don't want to lose that yet.*

At least you know you're going to lose, says the Admin. She can really put the point in pointed.

"Carrie," says the lady firefighter, letting Steve off the hook. A small upturn to her mouth appears as well. She's starting to like him. Of course, she is. Look at him. Luckily, he put his shirt back on before she got here, or he'd have her phone and her Social Security numbers by now.

"Nice to meet you, Carrie. I'm Steve." He holds out his hand and Carrie shakes it. "Thank you for all your help here putting the fire out. It was a relief to see the fire truck appear."

"I was relieved too," I tell Carrie. I also hold out my hand to shake hers, to get her to release Steve's hand. "I'm Gail." I say my name with some emphasis, hoping that Steve will remember that I'm still standing here.

"Steve and Gail, I know," Carrie tells us. "Peep told me that he showed you the tunnel to help you through. He asked me to give you a break." Carrie sees the hope in my face. "Don't worry," she tells me. "I won't turn you in, and I'll tell the others you're okay." I look to Steve to celebrate but he doesn't look at me. He's smiling at her. "We're all volunteers, so no one cares. They just want the fire out so they can get back to their lives."

"That's terrific. Thank you," says Steve to Carrie.

"Sure." Carrie shrugs her shoulders, then looks back at the tunnel. "Anyway, Peep and I have been concerned about the wiring in the tunnel and the fire hazard it's been for a long time. We've discussed plans to replace it together but hadn't found the time yet. I guess we'll find the time now."

"You and Peep stay in touch then?" asks Steve, who is wondering the same thing I am – maybe she and Peep are an item. I'm elated. Steve looks deflated. Then the tables turn.

"Peep is my brother," Carrie tells Steve. Wow, look at him beam. "Officially, you're still standing on our family property, even though you're in Canada. The Canadian government recognizes our owner-ship, which wasn't hard since our family has been living here since somewhere around forever. Now I'm the one who lives here."

"It must be nice to live here," says Steve to Carrie, in a dreamy voice.

"Yes, well…" I try to interject but am at a loss for what to say, until I look at our car. "What do we think of the car? Is it safe to drive?"

"I'm glad we got the insurance," says Steve. The car is riddled with dents and scratches on the passenger's side where the flying debris of broken barrels hit. The front passenger window is broken. Steve walks over and carefully removes the camouflage curtain from the windshield and hood. Carrie follows and helps him. Why didn't I think to follow and help him? The front corners of the car are smashed in from me plowing through the barrels. The headlights are gone, the hood is crumpled in the front, and the windshield has rivers of cracks winding through it. I'm glad we got the insurance.

"To answer your question, Gail, I don't think the car is safe to drive. I also think we'd get pulled over in a second if we did try to drive this," Steve tells me.

"What happens when we call for a tow and the car rental company knows we're in Canada?" I ask.

"I know a mechanic on the US side who can tow you," says Carrie. "We went to high school together. I can ask him to come through the tunnel and tow this back through. You can call in your report from his garage."

"Thanks," I reply, trying hard to sound grateful to the woman I wish would go away. Sure, she put out the fire we started, is keeping us out of jail, and is now saving us with the car rental company, but really – how much of this shiny angel should a regular woman have to take?

"Yes, thanks," says Steve. "Thing is, we're sort of on a mission to get to Vancouver tonight."

"Are you going to the Celebration of Light Festival?" asks Carrie. "It's Vietnam tonight."

"That's exactly what we're doing," Steve confirms. "We set off to do this without checking that Gail had her passport. It was very spur of the moment."

"Sounds like it," Carrie says. "Is there a neighbor or someone who has your house key who could fax you a copy of Gail's passport?"

"It's a long story that I'm not sure how to tell, but I can't really ask for help from home," I tell Carrie.

"Steve can't ask either?" Carrie continues.

"Gail and I just met today," explains Steve, "so no one in her home knows me. Her husband would probably call the police if a strange guy called up asking for her passport."

"Her husband?" Carrie looks to me and then to Steve with this question. "The two of you aren't married?"

"No!" says Steve, a little too emphatically, crushing my soul.

"Oh," says Carrie, now with some suspicion in her voice.

"We're just friends!" Steve jumps to add. "We met this morning in our dentist's office and decided to go on a small adventure today that we both needed. We're just stepping outside our norm. I think for us both it's well outside our norm to do something like this with a complete stranger as well." Steve put an emphasis on the word 'complete,' crumpling my crushed soul. Carrie looks at me for confirmation. What am I supposed to say?

"Yep, we're just friends on a trip who started as complete strangers this morning." I speak these words with a hushed tone that make them sound weak, like I might be lying. I guess it's because I'd rather they weren't true. I've lost any claim Carrie thought I may have had on Steve. Steve doesn't take any notice.

"Do you think your friend would be okay to tow our car tonight to his garage and then have us meet him there in the morning?" asks Steve.

Carrie pulls a phone out of her pocket and starts dialing. "I can ask." Carrie doesn't move away to make her call, and this frustrates me. I want a private moment to check in with Steve. I want to plan our next step without it involving Carrie. I can tell he hopes she'll be involved, however.

Let him involve her, instructs the Admin. *It's better for you both that she's here. Your feelings are getting out of hand.*

Can't I just have today for me? Can't I keep his attention on me for the rest of today then go back to my life tomorrow? I beg the Admin.

You were thinking of telling him how you feel, remember? And what's so wrong with your life? We have yet to establish that, the Admin counters. *You make it sound like going back to your life is like going back to prison to finish a life sentence.*

I think about this statement. I think about it hard. I decide it isn't fair. *My life isn't a prison. It's not that bad. I love John and I love our boys. My hardship is me. I don't like who I have to be all the time to keep our life going. I don't like what my job takes from me every day I'm there. Even on my days off, I don't stop working. I'm all work and no play. Today I'm playing, and I get Steve as my playmate. For this one day I just want to play.*

Get over yourself. Steve deserves a playmate that's right for him. You don't get to be Steve's playmate and maintain your innocence when you explain this to John. Get over it and help Steve out, especially after all he's done for you today, lectures the Admin.

Now you're taking Steve's side? These are the moments when I wish I could shove you or hit you. He's been the devil all day, according to you, and now you're defending him. Is it that important to you that you prove me wrong at every turn over everything?

I let out a very frustrated and angry exhale that catches Steve and Carrie by surprise. "I'm sorry." I say to them both. "I just felt a sharp pain in my neck. I'm okay, really." Carrie and Steve give me looks of concern for a short second, then return their attention to Carrie's phone. "I guess my friend isn't picking up his phone right now," says Carrie.

You know I'm right. The Admin decides to get the last word. *This pain in your neck is right. You agree with me that he deserves Carrie, and she's better for him than you are, and that kills you more than anything else I've said today.*

Dammit. The Admin is right, again.

"His voicemail is picking up now," says Carrie. "Hi, Fred, it's Carrie. I have a favor to ask. There's a wrecked car on my side of the family tunnel that I need you to tow back through to your garage. Please call my mobile." With that, Carrie hangs up.

"The tunnel seems less of a secret than I thought it was," I say to Carrie. "The other firefighters don't seem shocked that it's here, and your friend Fred is in on it too."

"Our neighbors know our secret, and we know they'll help us keep it. It's the beauty of living in a small town area. Even the neighbors who don't like us would still choose keeping the secret over talking to an outsider. You two are the first exception I know of to the rule."

From the tunnel we hear a motor. It isn't coming fast, but it's loud. Carrie looks like she recognizes the motor and starts walking toward the tunnel. I can't imagine Fred could get here that fast, and I'm right. From the charred mouth of the tunnel, Peep emerges on his yellow motorcycle, parking it a few feet outside the tunnel. Carrie greets him as he's removing his helmet.

"Hey, Peep, what do you think?" Carrie asks.

"I think our job of clearing the roots in the tunnel just got easier," Peep replies. He looks around at the spray of barrel pieces that litter the ground. "We lost the barrels, though. I liked having those old barrels." Peep looks over at us. "Are you okay?"

"We're okay," Steve answers. "Sorry about the tunnel, and the barrels. It's my fault." I start to correct him, but Peep jumps in first.

"No one's hurt. That's what matters." Peep sees our car, or what's left of it. "What are you going to do now?"

"I called Fred to come out and tow them back through to his garage," explains Carrie.

"Oh," says Peep. Then he looks over to me and Steve again. "What about getting to Vancouver to see the fireworks?"

"We were just starting to talk about that," I tell him. "We're not sure yet what happens next."

"Carrie, let them borrow your car," Peep says to his sister. Carrie gives Peep a look of exasperation. She's not into that idea.

"Excuse me?" is Carrie's hot reply.

"Come on, Carrie. They've come a long way for this. They'll be back tonight to return it. Nellie trusted them enough to tell them about the tunnel. I trust them too. They can get to the show in time to see it, then bring back your car before midnight." Peep turns to Steve and I. "When you guys get back, you can stay in the family home you met me in tonight. It's just a thirty minute walk from Carrie's house."

"Peep, the last car these two were in doesn't look so good. No offense," Carrie says to us over her shoulder.

"None taken," says Steve.

I'm about to pipe up that it isn't our first wreck today, but then I decide to keep quiet. Carrie and Peep lean into a sibling huddle where a battle of whispers and clipped hand movements begin. If we can borrow Carrie's car, then we may make it to Vancouver. Reaching Vancouver feels like reaching the Emerald City now. After all we've been through, I wonder if there's a mighty wizard there with a balloon to get us home later. Or a nice witch who tells me that clicking the heels of the red flats I'm wearing will put me back in my front yard. It's taken more than I could have imagined to reach a city that we should have reached in ninety minutes by plane. I think back on all the stops along the way. The yellow brick road to Vancouver has had many twists and turns. The perils we've survived make the Flying Monkeys look tame to me now. And yet, this is a journey I would not have missed for the world.

I look to Steve and realize I'm missing the chance to be alone with him again, if even for a moment. I step in front of him to get his attention, putting myself between him and her. Steve looks down at me to see what I need. It feels good to have him look at me. "It doesn't look like she wants to lend us her car," I say to him. "Maybe we can take a bus or call a cab?" Steve's shoulders slump a bit at this suggestion.

"I guess so," Steve says. "It would be easier and faster to get to Vancouver and back if we could borrow a car."

"Sure," I agree, not happy about it.

"Plus, it will help us get around when we get there if we have a car. I don't know where we're going in Vancouver, and it's a big city."

"True," I agree again, still not happy.

"Also, I think it will help if Carrie comes with us." There it is. "I'll bet she knows her way around." Steve makes this suggestion with as much innocence as he can muster.

"You like her," I tell him. "You're attracted to her." Steve looks down at me like he wants to play it off, but he can see that I know I'm right.

"Okay, yes, I like her. She's beautiful, and she's a firefighter, which doesn't get much sexier 'cause it's so damn cool, and she seems pretty amazing overall, so, yeah, I like her." Steve does a side step past me, so I'm not blocking him anymore. "They're done talking."

Carrie turns around to look at us. I can tell she doesn't know what to think of us. Truth be told, neither do I.

"I am going to drive you to Vancouver in my car," Carrie announces. "I don't know you, so I can't just hand you the keys. My brother, Peep here, says we should help you out, so I'm going to help you out." With that, Carrie walks over to another firefighter who has been putting equipment away in the fire truck, and Peep walks over to us.

"Don't worry about her. She's always happy to help someone. She just hates when the good ideas are mine," Peep tells us.

"I'm glad you think we're a good idea," says Steve.

"Me too," I say to Peep. "Thanks again."

"You're too close not to get to Vancouver. It's only an hour away. You'll make it in time to see the show, then Carrie will bring you back. It's no skin off her nose, really, so don't pay any attention to any attitude she may give you," Peep tells us.

"She's about to chauffeur two strangers for the evening who burned out a family landmark and thoroughly wrecked a car they don't own. I can understand a little attitude," says Steve.

Peep straightens up at these words. "I got my sister to give you a ride. I'm not setting you up with her. You wouldn't want her anyway. She snores like a bear."

Carrie finishes her conversation with the other firefighter and then rejoins us. Peep has a fixed stare of suspicion on Steve.

"Okay, we're good to go. Everything is done here. Come on," Carrie says to Steve and I as she gives Peep a quick hug. "My house is five minutes away, and we'll pick up my car there."

"Did you walk here in a fire suit?" ask Steve.

"I ran here in a fire suit. We all have to be in shape."

Steve gives Carrie a look showing how impressed he is, which causes her to smile as she turns to hug Peep good-bye. As soon as she faces away, Steve's look turns hungry. I can tell he's imagining what's under the fire suit. Peep can tell too. Peep's suspicious gaze on Steve is indignant at first, then fierce. As soon as Steve sees the daggers Peep is shooting at him, he makes a small cough, waves at Peep, and then turns around to me. It makes me feel good that Peep is on my side. Hopefully, Steve will take Peep's warning to heart and stop mooning over a person he has to say good-bye to in a few hours anyway.

How about you just concern yourself with your own selfish mooning over a man you have to say good-bye to in a few hours as well? the Admin pesters me.

I know when this journey ends, I tell her.

Are you going to let John know that you won't be home tonight? the Admin asks with a decided sneer.

I've been avoiding this thought for a long while. John doesn't deserve the worry my not coming home tonight will cause him. I have to call.

You have to call, the Admin orders me.

I will, I tell her. *After the fireworks, I'll call him and tell him everything. After the fireworks.*

Sure you will.

CHAPTER 23

*L*ike the gentleman his is, Steve puts himself in the back seat when we get in the car with Carrie. It is nice of him. I know he'd rather be up front with her. I could have been a good friend and insist he sit up front since his legs are longer, to help him out. I just don't want to do that.

Carrie keeps quiet for most of our ride. Steve tries to prompt conversation with her, but Carrie's brief responses are making it hard on him. I like her a bit more now.

"When did you move into your Canadian home?" Steve asks Carrie.

"After college," Carrie replies.

"What did you study in college?" Steve asks her.

"Architecture," Carrie replies.

"An architect? How interesting. Is that your career now?" Steve asks.

"It is," Carrie replies.

"Wow, have you designed buildings?" Steve continues on, hoping she'll tell a story about something she's done.

"Yes, it's what I do as an architect," Carrie replies.

Quiet. Steve doesn't know what more to say. Good, it was getting embarrassing. I look back at him. He looks deflated again, with his eyes down.

"I studied European literature," I tell them. "It didn't become a career for me, which I'm sure doesn't surprise anyone. I'm not sure why I studied it, except that I love to read and reading European literature made me feel more worldly and well read." No one says anything. I thought that was funny.

Now who's embarrassing? chimes the Admin.

Shut up, I tell her.

Two or three minutes pass with no one talking. The silence is a solace for me. The mood in the car is kind of tense, which may make for a long ride, but I don't mind. I guess Carrie starts to mind, however, because she locates her tongue and begins chatting.

"I designed a new city hall building for my town. It was my first big contract win. They liked my design ideas, and the price I bid, so I got to design the city hall building."

"That's fantastic," says Steve.

"It feels good each time I drive by it," Carrie says. "Plus, my work on the city hall is what launched my career. All of my subsequent work has come from that job. I can drive us by it on the way."

"I'd love to see it!" says Steve. And they're off. I'm not sure what changed Carrie's mood. I guess she decided to give Steve a break. They're conversing freely, and I might as well be invisible.

Good, be invisible, says the Admin. *You'll go watch these stupid fireworks, then we'll finally go home and resume a life that makes sense.*

You know what? I'm getting sick of you telling me that all the time. I know my life makes sense. I don't need you to tell me I have all I should have, and I do all I should do to keep it going. I shouldn't have to chant fifty times a day that I'm grateful when I'm not happy. I'm glad I did something for me today. I want to do more. I want to figure out how to be responsible for all I have in my life that I love, and be responsible for creating something in my life for me too.

I wait for a response from the Admin. *Nothing to say?* I ask her. I was expecting some kind of challenge or to be belittled, but the Admin has stepped away. That's a nice change.

While Steve and Carrie get to know each other, I start designing new pants for my boys in my head. They need pants that are sturdy in the knees. They're so rough on their pants. Maybe if I make panels out of duck cloth to reinforce the knees, then the pants will last longer. It's worth a try. I have duck cloth left over from the curtains I made for their room. Using curtain material in my kids' pants makes sense somehow. They need pants that last more than two weeks in the knees. My mind starts working on the patterns I'll make that will incorporate stronger panels into a pair of pants without them looking like the patches my mom used to sew over the knees of my pants when I was a kid. Those patches made me look like a hobo.

CHAPTER 24

*H*igh in the sky, John sits in the long viewing cabin of a zeppelin that was designed in the 1940s for first-class travelers. It even has a bar. Sheriff Tracy brought drinks to share and has manned the bar herself, mixing simple cocktails or pouring wine. At some point, she set what looks like a martini in front of John, but he hasn't had the desire to touch it. Huddled around the bar is Sheriff Tracy, Nellie, Edgar, and Edward, this craft's owner, all plotting how they can get the attention of Gail and Steve in the middle of a fireworks show and then get them on board this dirigible.

None of this would be possible without Ned's cousin Edward. It seems the Boeing family has a penchant for non-military aircraft from a wartime era. Edward's airway connections are making the whole trip possible, including picking up Nellie and Edgar in Portland, which was an interesting feat. That Nellie works in an airport helped, of course. John can't imagine what the logistics would have been otherwise because circling this zeppelin around the Portland airport and coming down low enough so Nellie and Edgar could climb on board was daring enough.

The suggestions John is hearing now on how they plan to get Gail and Steve on board from the middle of a crowd of thousands could rival Cirque du Soleil's bold choreography. Sheriff Tracy looks like she could spontaneously combust from all her excitement over this mission. John, on the other hand, sinks deeper into his chair, and into his fear, as they get closer to Vancouver. His world was clear this morning. Everyone looked good. The most pressing task in John's world was to get a robot arm to hold a pouch of champagne without bursting it in someone's face. Now his wife is in another country with another man.

"John, penny for your thoughts," Edgar says as he sits in a plush arm chair next to John. John looks into Edgar's eyes for a clue to what he should say next, then shakes his head a bit and looks out the window. John sees his own reflection look back at him in the glass and is reminded of how much his oldest son looks like him. Gail says so all the time. "I should just call her now."

"You could call her and tell her where you are, ask her what's going on. However..." Edgar looks over to the crowd of schemers as they put the final touches on their plan.

John's eyes follow Edgar's. "However, the flamboyant plans of Zelda the zeppelin's crew will go unrealized, and I'll spoil everyone's fun. How selfish of me."

"No, you should call Gail," says Edgar. "I can see the ocean of stress that's drowning you. Call her so you keep from losing your mind."

John takes his phone out of his pocket and does what he's done a hundred times today. He looks at Gail's dot in the locator service. She isn't far from Vancouver. Her and that guy stopped for a while at the border, but they're moving again. She'll get there in time for the show, same as John. John's thumb lingers over the phone, ready to speed-dial Gail. He looks at her dot. He's going to see her soon. If everything everyone has said about that guy and Gail is true, then John can swoop into Vancouver and surprise her – literally sweep her off her feet. If there's more going on with Gail and... well, maybe he didn't have to rush to find that out. John puts the phone back in his pocket.

"Changed your mind," Edgar observes.

"Yeah, changed my mind."

"Do you want something else to drink? I can get you a beer or a soda if the martini isn't what you want," offers Edgar.

"No, thanks," says John. "Edgar, when you saw Gail this morning, you saw something in her that made you convince her to do this, to take this trip. Was she so sad to you?"

Edgar thinks on his encounter with Gail this morning and the brief conversation they had outside the ladies' restroom in his restaurant. "I wouldn't say she was sad. I would say she looked lost. She looked like she needed some light to help her see her way again. I also know what Steve has been through in the past year. I thought that getting out of the city and helping someone like Gail could help him too."

"I don't care what's happened to him," John says with brewing anger.

"Okay," says Edgar. "I'm sorry. I didn't mean to hurt you with talk of…"

"You know, I think I know what happened. You talked my wife into going off with him because you thought you could do something for him that would make him notice you, because you have a crush on him." These words tumble out of John, and they feel good. His anger has a target.

"I tried not to let my feelings get in the way. His wife died, John," Edgar says.

"So you offered him mine?!" John jerks himself forward so he's sitting bolt upright, ready to battle Edgar over what he has done.

"Take a breath, John." Edgar tries to soothe him but also distance himself, pressing his back into his chair. "Please, take a breath. Take a sip of your drink. Calm down and listen to me."

John wakes to his posture and sees he's scared Edgar. It isn't easy, but he manages to move himself back so he doesn't look ready to pounce. John reaches for his drink with concerted effort and focus. He manages to bring the drink to his lips and take a sip. Focusing his attention on the drink helps to calm him. After another sip, John returns the glass to the table and takes in a breath before raising his eyes to meet Edgar's. "I'm sorry," John says in a near whisper.

"It's okay," says Edgar. "Your day hasn't been an easy one. John, I hope in our short time together that I've earned a little trust." Edgar waits for a response.

John thinks through his time with Edgar and all that Edgar has done to help him today. This thread of thought helps him stop pointing his anger at Edgar and nod in agreement.

"Good, thank you. I want you to know that I didn't mean to cause harm. That you're hurting and scared weighs on me. I want to get you to Gail as soon as possible so this hurt will stop because I do believe it will stop when you see her. In my heart, John, I don't believe Gail is running from you or her life with you. I believe she's running to find Gail. I'm glad I will get to see what today has done for her. She went down in a plane, John, and she didn't give up. She's still on her way to Vancouver. She's doing this for her. I think you're going to like what you see when we find her."

John has a tough time envisioning Gail as lost. Gail is forever focused on what needs to happen each day to keep their lives running. She's the person everyone turns to when something needs to get done, at home and at work. She's the person friends and family talk to when they need help, any kind of help: personal, financial, work, or relationships. She takes care of it all. How can she be lost? Gail is the finder of anything lost in the house, and the guide for anyone looking lost on the street.

Sure, they don't get out like they did before kids. Most nights, John and Gail watch TV and drink wine before going to bed. That's all they do really as entertainment these days. Maybe she needs to get out and have more fun. John is more than willing to get out of the house and have more fun with Gail. Of course, this is assuming that he's still the man she wants to have fun with. He feels a flare of hurt from the open sucking wound that the fear harpoon left behind. For a moment, he forgot about the hurt and fear. John hopes he gets the chance to fix whatever needs fixing with Gail.

"We're not far now," announces Sheriff Tracy. John sees she is looking at him with a great deal of concern. He looks around and sees that everyone is looking at him with concern. His outburst at Edgar seems to have caught everyone's attention.

"Thanks," John says to the sheriff. Then he shifts to face the entire crew, "Thanks, everyone, for all you're doing to help me find Gail. From what I heard of your plan, I think it'll be an impressive display for the crowd, and for Gail."

This brings everyone back to their excitement. "Would you like to hear all the details we've figured out?" asks Sheriff Tracy. "I'm so excited about my part!"

"Sure," says John. "Lay it on me."

Sheriff Tracy, Nellie, Edward, and Edgar gather around John to boast over all they've divined. John tries to hear them, but his mind wanders up to the forward cabin where Ned sits piloting the zeppelin. John wonders if he can find a way to be up there in the pilot's cabin. He's sure it's quiet with Ned.

CHAPTER 25

*W*e drive into Vancouver with no trouble at all. It seems odd to me that there isn't some obstacle to getting into the city. A troll should be waiting at the entrance to challenge us with a riddle we must solve or die. Walls that are thirty feet tall and ten feet thick should be surrounding the city, forcing us to find a secret entrance. But before we can find the secret entrance, we have to win the trust of an ancient hermit living at the back wall so he gives us the location and the key to unlock it. That is more the kind of greeting I expected when approaching our final destination after the day we've had. Instead, we're driving in as the sun is setting on our day, and it's all very nice. We're enjoying a beautiful sunset view of the ocean, with mountains in the distance. We pass large parks full of happy people. The weather is clement, for Pete's sake. There's nothing wrong. Why do I feel so let down?

Nothing is ever good enough for you, the Admin pokes at me. *You drag us all the way here and now you're not happy, again. Priceless.*

I'm sure the fireworks will be great, I say to the Admin, with half-hearted enthusiasm. The Admin rolls her eyes for the hundredth time today. I hate when she rolls her eyes at me. I try not to notice. This time, though, her eye roll captures how I'm feeling better than anything I could say myself. I should be thrilled that we're here. All I feel is tired. I look back at Steve and see that he's staring through his window at Vancouver. He looks a little confused.

"What do you think, Steve?" I ask him.

"About what?" he answers.

"About Vancouver," I say.

"I like Vancouver. It's not my first time here, remember?" he tells me.

"I know," I say. "I was just wondering what you're thinking as you enter Vancouver this time, after the day we've had."

"Oh," he says. "It seems quiet."

"Yeah, it does seem quiet." I agree. "It's a strange feeling of quiet."

"Well, it won't be quiet for long," Carrie warns us. "In about five minutes we'll be on the outskirts of the event space. I'll get you as close as I can, then you'll need to walk in with your tickets."

"Thanks, Carrie," says Steve. "Thanks again for getting us to the event. I was afraid outside the tunnel that we'd miss it."

"Sure," Carrie says. She doesn't look as put out with us as she did at the start of this car ride. I'm glad, especially since she's our ride out of here. "Okay, here we go," Carrie leans forward a bit over her steering wheel.

We've turned a corner to see large groups of people walking in the same direction, smiling and chatting, carrying blankets and water bottles. We must be close now. Another couple of blocks in, and people are starting to walk in the street in front of and around our car. We're not the only car, but the pedestrians have the cars outnumbered and are making it hard to proceed.

"Go ahead and jump out," Carrie instructs us. "I'm going to head back three blocks and wait at a coffee shop for you. You have my number, so call when you're out again, and we'll find each other."

"Thank you, Carrie," says Steve as he opens his door and gets out.

"Yes, thank you," I say to her as I move to open my door.

"You're welcome, Gail. Good luck."

"I don't think we'll have any trouble," I tell her. "We just walk in and watch fireworks from here."

"I didn't mean good luck with the event. I just meant good luck," Carrie says.

"Okay, thanks," I say to her, then open my door. What was that about? Steve has come around to my side of the car. He holds the door for me as I get out and then leans in for a last good-bye to Carrie.

"Thanks again, Carrie. See you later." Steve smiles to her.

"Sure," I can hear her say as Steve closes the car door. He waves and smiles to her again before straightening up and looking at me.

"Ready?" Steve asks me with a big grin of triumph on his face.

"Yes," I tell him. "Let's do this." We start walking in the same direction as those around us. Before we get too far away from Carrie and are absorbed by the crowd, Steve turns around for one last wave at her.

"You're like a schoolboy you're so excited over her," I tell him.

"Am I?" Steve asks with a smile. "It feels good to be interested in someone. I can't tell if she has any interest in me, though."

"She'd be a blind idiot not to be interested in you." I poke at him like a little sister, or the dear friend I guess I'm relegated to be now. Steve gives me the biggest grin I've seen from him. The crowd is getting thick now as we approach a blockade set out across a street entrance. There are gates with people taking tickets. This is it. We're entering the Emerald City. Steve reaches down and grabs my hand. I know he's grabbed it so we don't get separated, but his touch ignites my hand and spreads happiness all over and through me.

Settle down, the Admin orders me.

Let me enjoy this, I fire back at her. *Nothing is going to happen between me and Steve. That much is obvious after our ride with Carrie.*

You're letting something happen now, the Admin states. *It's wrong for you to hold his hand if you're going to orgasm from it.*

I'm not about to orgasm, I tell her. *It feels good. That's it. I'm allowed to feel good.*

You get to feel good when I say you can, rules the Admin. *You're going back to your life after this little show, don't forget. You have a lot to do to make up for today. First on the list is doing everything you can to save your marriage after John hears all that you did today.*

John will understand, I say to the Admin. *I think he'll understand.*

Would he understand if he saw you now? Holding the hand of a man he doesn't know? asks the Admin.

No, he wouldn't. He wouldn't understand if he saw me now. I'm not sure he'd recognize me if he saw me now. This thought doesn't make me happy.

Exactly, jabs the Admin. *You're not this selfish person that you've let yourself be today. You take care of everyone. That's what you do.*

It's not as easy as it used to be, I tell her. *It's too much now. Even when I try to rest I'm not resting. I'm planning out what happens next at work, at home, with the kids, with the bills, with taxes, with the shopping...*

"Tickets." A person wearing a headset with a walkie-talkie on her belt is looking at me. I'm disoriented. I wasn't watching where we were. Steve drops my hand to reach his back pocket and pulls out our tickets. The ticket lady takes them and holds them under a UV light. Bright lines that end in sparkles appear. The fireworks display on the tickets satisfies the ticket lady that they're real. She gives them back to us and tells us to move ahead to the next station, where a person checks through my purse then lets us in.

We're in. We're here. We're at the end. We're going to see fireworks, and then we're going home. I feel sick. I look around and see a bank of portable toilets with a short line of people in front of them. "I need to use the bathroom," I tell Steve.

"Yeah, me too," Steve says.

We get in line, and my stomach and bowels are erupting. My whole body feels like it could seize up or explode. I'm only one person away from the toilets, but the pressure in my bowels makes me question if I'll make it. I can feel the pulse in my temples. Thankfully, two toilets open at the same time. I get in and get seated just in time. My whole body wrenches in on itself. For a moment, I think I may need to turn around and vomit, which I really don't want to do in a portable toilet. I take slow, deep breaths. The moment passes. I think of John. I think of going home to John. This thought settles me some. I miss him. I want to tell him about today. I want him to see me.

Then it happens. Clarity springs into view. I know what I need to do. I'm afraid for what it will mean, but it has to happen now. Watching the fireworks and then going home to my life won't mean what it needs to unless I take care of this business first. My stomach wants to flare up in protest, but I tell myself to hold it together. The next few minutes are going to be the most important ones of the day. I leave the toilet and look around. I see Steve and he sees me.

"Hey, are you okay? You look like you're about to cry," he says.

"I'm okay," I say. I reach out and take his hand. Instead of a spark up my arm, the connection this time is calming. "Before we go further, I need a few minutes to myself. There's something I need to do for me, and I need to do it right now so I can enjoy the fireworks and then whatever it is that happens next for me."

"Okay," he says with caution. I can see he doesn't get it.

"This will only take a few minutes. I'm not going to go far." I look around and see a small cluster of trees off the path of people. I point to the trees so Steve sees them too. "I'm going to be right there next to those trees. I won't move from that spot. How about you get us some water and food and meet me over there?"

"You're not going to run out on me, right?" I can see he's trying to joke but has genuine concern.

I smile up at Steve with a determined look that says I am not going anywhere. "No. I just need a moment to myself. I'll be right there at those trees waiting for you, I promise."

Steve looks reassured. "Okay, sure, I'll go get water and some food. Is there anything I should or should not buy you to eat?"

"I'll eat anything, thanks," I tell him. Steve gives my hand a squeeze, then drops it and walks off in search of food. I watch him for a moment, then turn to the trees. It's hard to get my feet to move toward them. I take a breath and hold it. I let it out and force my feet to move. I'm not sure what I want to say. I search for words as I navigate between a stream of people to the small grotto off the path. When I get there, the Admin is waiting.

You know you can't do this, the Admin tells me.

I know I have to try, I reply. I look up into her face and take in how beautiful she is to me. She's taller than me. Her features are as striking as they are severe. She is confident and strong. I've always seen her as better than me. This is the problem.

Today has helped me see that I can do much more than I thought I could. Please understand, I try to explain to her.

You don't pick out your shoes each day without me. How can you possibly imagine that this one day has changed everything you and I have built?

I know that everything is the same at home and at work and that I'm going back to what you and I have created. None of that will have changed. What has changed today is me. I have changed. These words land hard on the Admin. I can see her reeling and ready to fire back.

Listen to me. Just listen... remember what Sheriff Tracy said to me before I went up the ladder to the trapeze? I was so laser-focused on her I think I may have memorized her words. She said, "It goes against all of what your mind and body thinks is right for you to do, but those are just ideas. Know that you're safe. Know that you're with the right people in this moment. What you can't know is what happens next until you let it happen. You can't know what this will mean to you until you've tried." I have to try to live my life without you.

Before I do, though, I need to tell you, I need to say thank you. Thank you, my Admin, for watching over me and being strong for me when I couldn't be strong for myself. Thank you for being my confidence and my guide. Thank you for loving me in the best way you knew how – in the only way either of us knew. You kept me organized, and you kept me moving when I had stopped dead inside. I don't think I have words to express how grateful I am. I reach out and hug my Admin. I bring her close to me and grip her with all my strength so she knows I mean what I'm saying. I can feel her melt into my embrace. I can feel her hug me back. She sees that I'm ready. Once again, she's giving me support when I need it.

Thank you, Admin. I love you. You're fired.

The words leave me and the deed is done. Inside a heartbeat, my Admin fades away. For the first time in a long while, I am standing on my own. I tell myself I'm going to be okay, and I believe it.

The crowd is getting thicker around me. It's odd to think that I can be near so many people who have no idea what a monumental change

I've just made for myself. I lean against a tree and marvel at what I've done today. I can't wait to get my hands on my sewing machine.

A few minutes pass, and I see Steve's head moving toward me. The view of his head makes me giggle. It's like a bobbing apple moving over water. Steve bobs his head higher to tell me he can see me. This is too much, and I start laughing out loud. It startles those around me, but I don't care. I wave and smile at people and tell them to have a great time. People smile back and return my greeting. This all feels so good. As Steve emerges from the sea of people and reaches my grotto, I see he has a couple of wrapped food items in one hand and two water bottles in the other.

"Well, not only are you still here," says Steve, "but you look thoroughly happy. In fact, I would say you are radiant right now. Can I ask what you've been doing these last few minutes?"

"I let go of what I don't need anymore," I tell him, with what I can feel is a glowing smile. "I think if I tried to explain it you would think I'm crazy, so let's just eat."

"Alright," says Steve. He hands me a wrapped item and a bottle of water. "It's a loaded burrito. You said you'd eat anything."

"That's perfect, thank you," I peel back the foil at one end and start diving into the warm food. This is maybe the best burrito I've ever had.

"Let's eat and walk, if that's okay. It's going to take us a while to get through the crowd to our viewing area."

With a mouth full of burrito I nod in agreement, and we shuffle our way between people until we're midstream and moving with the flow. Steve and I stay elbow to elbow with each other.

Excitement for the fireworks is building in me. I'm about to see a world-class display of explosive light and sound, put on by people from a country I've only read about or heard about on TV. Vietnam seems so far away, yet this team is here in Canada with hundreds of pounds of fireworks they've choreographed into what I'm sure will be a stunning display.

I can see out onto the bay, where boats are floating with partying passengers ready to catch the show from what has to be a terrific viewing spot. From what I can tell, the fireworks must happen over the bay. I'm a little jealous of the people on the water – what a great way to see it all. I feel certain they have the best view until a helicopter catches my attention. I look up into the sky and watch as it flits over buildings and circles the crowd. I can see small planes moving around in the sky as well. I tug on Steve's sleeve, so he bends his ear toward me. I point to one of the planes and ask him, "I wonder if those are allowed to fly around up there during the show?"

"What a great view that would be," Steve says. "I wish I had my plane. Though, if I got to choose I think I'd want to be up in that." I follow Steve's finger and see a blimp in the sky. It's shaped like a silver bullet.

"How fantastic would that be?" I almost scream.

"It would be pretty fantastic, I'm sure," Steve agrees.

Meanwhile, up in the sky...

CHAPTER 26

*J*ohn is terrified. Everyone is so confident about this plan. He can't imagine they can pull this off without someone getting hurt. Sheriff Tracy is in a harness, for crying out loud. She is talking excitedly to Edgar and Nellie, going over the plan one last time before they all swing into action.

Edward, who has been up front with Ned, rejoins them in the main cabin to give the group his report. "I just got off the phone with the air traffic controller for the event. He's cleared our plan with the mayor of Vancouver. We have twenty minutes before the Vietnam team starts their show."

Everyone checks their watches. They've become a synchronized team on a mission. That they're in a World War I-era zeppelin seems all the more appropriate to John.

Edward continues his briefing, "We have to leave the air space in less than twenty minutes. Ned is bringing us over to the edge of the bay, where the mayor has his platform."

John walks over to a window and locates the platform. "I think I can see the platform," he announces. "We're close." John takes out his phone and looks at his locator app. "Gail is here. Her dot is along the edge of the bay."

"When will the big board send our message?" Sheriff Tracy asks Edward.

"Any second now," Edward tells her.

* * *

"WE MADE IT!" Steve says to me as we reach our viewing area. We throw away our burrito wrappers and find a good spot to stand. The moment we stop walking, we exchange beaming looks of pride, then throw our hands straight up in victory and scream. People around us take our joy as excitement for the show and join in on the screaming.

Steve reaches down and picks me up into a bear hug. With my arms wrapped around his neck, we give each other a tight squeeze of gratitude. "We made it," Steve says again into my ear so I can hear him past the shouting around us.

"Thank you for bringing me here," I tell him.

"Thank you, Gail. I wouldn't be here without you either." Steve holds on to me for another few seconds, then gently puts me down.

"Gail?" I hear someone in the crowd say my name. "Harker. Gail Harker." I look around to see who is talking to me, but no one is looking at me or moving toward me. Then I hear a different voice in the crowd say, "Steve. Steve Wright?"

"Hello?" I call out to the crowd. "Who's looking for Gail and Steve?" Several people around us stare at me now. One woman catches my attention then extends her arm out and points to the bay. Others around her extend their arms out too and point in the same direction. I look at Steve as I turn to see what everyone around me is pointing to and notice that he is already looking in that direction and is fixated by what he sees. I follow his gaze to search for what has his and the crowd's attention, but I don't need to search for anything. Instantly, I see my name on a huge screen. My name looks three stories high: Gail. That one word, my name, fills the entire screen. Maybe it isn't me, I think, but then the screen blinks and my full name appears across it: Gail Harker. Another blink and it's Steve's turn. His name fills the screen: Steve. Blink: Steve Wright.

Blink: Gail Harker and Steve Wright. Make your way to the mayor's platform.

In front of the big screen, there is a platform and a podium. A man walks to the podium and waves to the crowd. Applause erupts around us. The crowd waves back and cheers for him as he speaks into the podium microphone. "Hello, friends and visitors! I am the mayor of Vancouver, and I am proud and thrilled to welcome you here for this year's Celebration of Light Festival!" The applause gets louder. People are shouting and hooting. "We have a few minutes before the show by Vietnam begins. Right now I need two special guests to make their way up here to this platform with me: Gail Harker and Steve Wright." I feel a nudge behind me. I turn to see the woman who first pointed me to the big screen behind me edging me forward.

"You two are Gail Harker and Steve Wright?" she shouts to me over the cheers and applause of the crowd.

"Yes," I shout back at her.

"Then that's where you need to go," she points to the big screen and the platform with the mayor in front of it. "That's the mayor's platform," she tells me, like she's explaining something simple to a child who doesn't get it. I must look as dazed as I feel. Steve grabs my arm to move us both toward the platform. I thank the woman, then follow Steve. His hand travels down my arm and grabs my hand. As he leads me through the crowd, I see the thick sea of people part before us. No one looks put out as we pass. People smile and ask us what we've won. I wish I knew. Then I remember we're here illegally. Would Carrie have ratted us out after all? I ask myself if we should run. The Admin would know what to do. I'm chagrined that I need her so soon but determined not to ask her back.

A few in the crowd shout ahead asking others to make a way for us so our passage is smooth. The mayor sees us coming and signals for us to make our way around the stage to its side so we can get up the stairs to the platform. It's too late to run, he's seen us, but I don't see any police waiting for us up there either. I look around at all the activity and attention around me. I let myself relax and get caught up in the excitement, so much so in fact that I'm oblivious to the four hundred ton gorilla hovering above me, until Steve points straight up at it.

* * *

JOHN AND EDWARD are watching the crowd as the big screen delivers their message. The rest of the team have taken their positions and are waiting to fly into action. The mayor is talking. John and Edward can hear him over a radio station Ned has piping through the speakers in the cabin. There is movement in the crowd. It looks like people are parting. John looks through a pair of binoculars and follows the line of parting people until he sees Gail. He sees her making her way to the platform. Gail is smiling and beautiful. John is elated that he's done what he set out to do today. He found his wife. The crowd thins out around her, and he sees she's holding someone's hand. The elation dissipates, allowing air to pass through the harpooned cavity in John's chest. He looks up the arm attached to the hand holding Gail's and sees him. Steve. Steve is also smiling and beautiful. A scraping pain gnaws at the cavity like a tumbleweed passing through the hole.

"Can you see them?" Edward asks John.

"Yes," he says quietly. "They're almost to the platform."

Edward rushes to the opposite side of the cabin and hurries down a flight of stairs as fast as his feet can carry him. At the bottom of the stairs is an open hatchway with another set of stairs below it. Edward lays himself on the floor, puts his head through the hatchway, and yells to Edgar, Nellie, and Sheriff Tracy below, "Alpha team, you are a go!" Edward then pushes himself back up to standing and runs up the stairs to John.

Edgar and Nellie and Sheriff Tracy wait, standing on a breezeway next to an armature built to hold a small aircraft docked for storage during one of the zeppelin's former World War I-era flights. There is no aircraft docked during this flight, but there is a winch on the armature strong enough to lasso in a thousand pounds or two of airplane when needed. Today the winch only needs to hold the weight of Sheriff Tracy plus one. The sheriff has shed her outer vestments to reveal her pink unitard once again. A full-body harness is strapped over her unitard, and she's wearing goggles. The sheriff turns her back to Edgar and Nellie so Edgar can hook her up. Edgar grabs the cable running from the winch. Nellie moves to the winch controls and presses a button to release enough tension on the cable for Edgar to carry it over to Sheriff Tracy and secure the heavy, locking hook at the end of the cable to the back of her harness. Edgar checks the lock on the hook four times to be sure it's secure before he drops the cable and walks around Sheriff Tracy to face her.

"You're in. The hook is securely locked. I checked it several times. Are you sure you still want to do this?" Edgar asks.

"Yes! Don't worry, Edgar, I'll be safe and so will they. Get the tandem harness." Edgar runs back to the hatchway stairs where another harness lays at its base. He picks it up and brings it over. They work together to affix the tandem harness to the front of her harness. When they're both certain the extra harness is secure, they turn to Nellie and each give her a thumbs up. Nellie nods and gives them a thumbs up back. Nellie works the winch controls, while Edgar keeps an eye on Sheriff Tracy and the daring transport of two extra passengers that is about to take place.

* * *

"LADIES AND GENTLEMEN, we have an unexpected pre-show event to attend to before Team Vietnam starts their show," the mayor announces to the crowd as Steve and I make our way onto the platform. As we approach him, the mayor turns halfway so he can see us but still speak into his microphone. "Gail and Steve, I presume?"

We both nod yes to the mayor. Steve holds out his hand to shake the mayor's. "Hi, yes, I'm Steve Wright, and this is Gail Harker."

"Hello, Steve," says the mayor, who then turns to me. "Hello, Gail, and welcome to Vancouver! I've heard a little about you and the trip you took to get here today." This is it. He's going to arrest us. I'm dumbfounded as to why he's being so nice about it.

The mayor turns to the crowd. "Steve and Gail are here from San

Francisco. They've been on a couple of plane rides and travelled hours by car to get here to see our Celebration of Light Festival." The mayor turns back to us. "I know the show tonight will be worth the trip, Gail and Steve. I also know you're going to enjoy the show even more when you're watching from this blimp hovering over us."

What did the mayor just say? I look up at Steve to ask him what the mayor means, but he looks down at me with the same question in his face.

The mayor continues, "Look up! Both of you look up. Your ride is here!"

I look up to see the blimp hasn't moved. It is still directly overhead. Then my eyes focus on something my mind won't believe. There's a woman on a string dangling from the blimp, and she's getting closer. She's more than halfway down from the blimp. I grab Steve's arm and point to the woman with my free hand.

"I see her!" says Steve. "Does that pink unitard look familiar to you?" I try to focus on the woman's face as she descends straight toward me. The woman waves at us with both hands. It isn't until I see her wide grin that I recognize her.

"That's Sheriff Tracy!" I yell at Steve, not taking my eyes off the wide grin.

"I know! I can't believe it!" Steve yells back at me.

Sheriff Tracy descends and lands gracefully on the platform within ten feet of us. We both move to greet her but she puts her hands up flat in front of her and tells us to wait. Then Sheriff Tracy takes a small jog in a circle where she stands, waving her arms up and down. Within a few seconds, the cable stops falling. Sheriff Tracy opens her arms wide to us and says, "Gail and Steve! Come here and hug me!" We both move in on Sheriff Tracy and hug her together.

"I can't believe it," I yell in her ear. "What on earth are you doing here?"

"I don't have time explain right now," our sheriff says. She pries herself free of us and then gets to work on the harness she's wearing. "Gail, I need you to put on this tandem harness. You're going to ride up with me to the zeppelin."

She can't be serious. I look at the harness she's working loose from her body, then I look up at the blimp overhead. "You know, I don't think so," I respond. "There's no way I can do that."

"Gail, you've flown through the air once today. You can do it again. As I recall, you were good at it, so this won't be a problem for you." Sheriff Tracy turns to Steve. "I'm more nervous about you, Steve, to be honest."

"I'm not offended. I'm nervous about me too," Steve replies. "Sheriff Tracy, this is an amazing gesture, but we can see the fireworks just fine from down here."

"Yes!" I agree excitedly. "I'm sorry to have you go back up alone, but…"

"Gail, John is up there," Sheriff Tracy tells me as she pulls the tandem harness away from her body and bends over, holding it open so I can step in.

"What did you say?" I ask her.

Sheriff Tracy straightens up and looks me in the eye to be sure I get what she's saying this time. "Your husband, John Harker, is up in that zeppelin. He's followed you from San Francisco. I don't have time to explain more than that. Right now, for his sake and yours, you need to get in this harness and ride up this cable with me. I wouldn't ask you to do this unless I knew it was safe. Now please hop to it and let's get going. I have to come back down for Steve."

Steve. I look to Steve to make sense of this for me. He seems to be wrapping his mind around Sheriff Tracy's words himself, then he takes my shoulders and turns me toward her.

"You first," he says in my ear. "I'll be right behind you. Step in."

Without thinking through what I'm doing, I step into the harness. My mind is on John. John is here. I'm going to see John. John's name and face fill my head. The thought of him is joyful and paralyzing. I'm not sure what will happen when I see him.

Sheriff Tracy, meanwhile, has flown into action, getting the tandem harness up and over my shoulders, strapping it through my legs and around my waist, cinching it tight. Then she turns me around so we're facing in the same direction. She moves in right behind me and gets to work clamping fasteners on her harness to metal loops around my shoulders, back, and waist. I feel her arms come around my waist and grip me tight. I can't imagine that her arms could hold my weight as we dangle up six or seven flights of air, but the feel of her hug reassures me just the same.

"You're perfectly safe, Gail. Enjoy the ride," Sheriff Tracy whispers in my ear. "Steve, run in a circle around us!"

Steve runs a circle around Sheriff Tracy and me. The cable on the ground next to our feet starts to lift. A moment later, my feet leave the platform. I grip Sheriff Tracy's arms out of instinct, and she tightens her hold on me in response. Within seconds, we're several feet off the ground and climbing. I shut my eyes. It's too much. I'm dangling like a worm on a fishing line. Luckily, there's no wind to bob us around on the line. I do think I would vomit on those nice people below me if we were to start bobbing around. The sound of the audience cheering grows faint as the ride continues. I can hear them, but they're getting further and further away. The sound of air rushing past my ears is louder now. It isn't wind. I'm not bobbing, but the sound of air is louder now than the sound of people.

"Isn't this beautiful, Gail? Are you looking all around? Take it in. You'll never see the world from this angle again," says my guardian angel sheriff.

I battle inside over whether I should open my eyes. I decide to trust my angel. I throw open my eyes like a scared child throws herself off a high diving board to overcome her fear. At once, I am overjoyed that I didn't miss this. Sheriff Tracy is right again. The city of Vancouver, its people and its lights, is all so beautiful. I can see the motion of the world below me, but where I am is still and quiet. I look out to where the water meets the horizon and see the great expanse of stars rise from the ripples of the bay. My eyes travel up, following the stars, taking in how they blanket us like gems of light. It seems a shame to me in this moment that the smoke from the fireworks will mask the stars soon.

Out of the top periphery of my gaze, I catch sight of the four hundred ton gorilla again. How do I keep losing sight of this mammoth aircraft? I'm not able to look straight up, or I'd crack Sheriff Tracy's nose behind me. I can see enough of the beast, however, and as we climb ever closer, it is all I can see around me.

"We're nearly to the breezeway below the zeppelin where I'll drop you off," Sheriff Tracy tells me.

I'm relieved and kind of sad that the ride is almost over. Then I remember why I took this ride. As we're lifted into the blimp's underbelly, I whip my head around, trying to focus through the metal supports and find John. We finally pass through the lower breezeway structure and are lifted through an opening to a series of walkways. When my head passes through an opening of floor, my eyes see a familiar pair of shoes waiting at the edge. As I travel up to our final stop, more of John is revealed to me until I'm able to see his face, his magnificent face, full of concern. John looks more scared than I've ever seen him. My arms shoot out, and I strain to get to him, to put my arms around him. John reaches out and grabs the harness strap at my waist and pulls me to him. My arms and legs clamber to wrap themselves around him. I hear Sheriff Tracy behind me saying, "Whoa! Hold on! Just a sec, you two," but it doesn't matter. I get my arms around John's neck and my legs around his waist and I grip him.

"I love you! I'm so glad you're here. I love you so much," I scream into his ear. My John is here and the day is complete. My love is here to share the final piece of the best day of my life.

"I love you, Gail. I love you," he yells back. We hold onto each other with fierce strength. Waves of happiness course through me. Then I feel another set of arms around me.

"I love you both too," Sheriff Tracy screams to us. "I know I just met you today, but you're both such wonderful people." She gives me and John a big squeeze, then releases us and starts to tug at my arms and legs. "As beautiful as this moment is, I need to get that harness off you and get back down the line."

John releases me and starts to work at a buckle at my waist. I allow my arms and legs to let him go and put my feet on the walkway. I feel the tension of the harness loosening around my shoulders where

Sheriff Tracy has unclamped me from her. John's fingers are working fast, but they don't manage to unbind me.

"May I?" I hear from behind John. "I can get her out of the harness in two seconds. I've been practicing all afternoon." With that, John moves to the side and reveals Edgar, my fairy spirit guide. I'm stunned.

"Crepes Fairy?" I stammer.

"Yes, my dear, it is I! I am here to reunite you and your lovely husband." Edgar has the harness off me before he finishes his sentence. He puts his hands on my shoulders and helps me move four steps to the side and back into John's arms. Edgar reattaches the harness to Sheriff Tracy before I'm able to blink twice. He tugs on the harness at several points to ensure it's on right. He flips Sheriff Tracy around and checks points on her harness and the clamp that connects her to the cable. He flips Sheriff Tracy back around so she's facing him again. "Are you ready?" he asks her. She gives him two thumbs up and a Cheshire Cat grin which convinces me she's more than ready to take the long carnival ride back down for Steve. Edgar moves a step to the side so he can see behind Sheriff Tracy and puts two thumbs up high over his head. I follow Edgar's gaze to see who he is signaling. There at the controls is our sandwich goddess and miracle provider, Nellie. How the freak did all this happen?

I watch as Sheriff Tracy is lowered down through the opening. Everyone is watching her intently. As soon as Sheriff Tracy's head is through the opening, Edgar lays down on the floor and keeps an eye on her.

I look over to Nellie and see that she has her eyes glued on Edgar. With my arms still wrapped around John, I tug at him to move us both over to Nellie. "Nellie? How did you get here?" I ask her.

"It's a strange and very interesting story that I'll tell you in ten minutes," she answers me. "Right now, I need to do this job. John, take Gail up to the cabin. We'll join you there as soon as Sheriff Tracy and Steve are on board."

Now it's John's turn to tug at me and move us to the stairs leading up and away from my landing pad. We take the stairs together and reach a glamorous open cabin with windows that let us see out at almost every angle around us. Steve was right. This is the best seat for the show. I look up to John to tell him how we saw the blimp before and talked about it, and to ask how he got here, but I'm stopped when I see tears rolling down his face.

"Are you okay?" I ask him.

"No," he snaps. "I'm happy that you're safe and here in my arms, and I'm so mad at you!" Anger takes over John's face, and his arms drop from around me. He turns and starts pacing a few feet in front of me. "Why, Gail?! Why did you take off with that guy and not say anything to me? Do you love him?"

"No, I love you. I'm so…"

"Don't apologize yet, I'm not through yelling at you. You left! You left me, and you left the country. You left our boys, and you didn't call to say why."

"I was coming back," I try to explain.

"Stop interrupting me!" John yells at me. "What was so wrong that you had to leave the country and not tell me, or not take me?" His rage turns to raw pain with these last words. My wonderful day has caused him a world of pain. "Why did you go with him and not me? Do you love him?" The tears are streaming down John's face. I wait to see if there's more he needs to say. I want to scream that I don't love Steve to ease his pain – and I realize it's true. I don't love Steve. Steve woke me up again to all the love I have, but I don't love him. Standing here with John sets every cell in my body on fire. I'm awake to this love again – our love, the love that came easy because this man I love is everything I've ever wanted, and more. And he feels the same for me.

"Tell me," John implores. "Tell me if you're in love with him."

"I'm not in love with him. I'm in love with you," I tell my husband.

"And?" he asks.

"And… I didn't call because I didn't know what to say. No, that's not right. I was afraid if I called you that I'd chicken out of the day and go home without seeing my adventure to its end. I also didn't want to hurt you. I failed miserably at that part, I can see, and I'm so sorry for that, but John, I'm not sorry I took off today. I did something for me, and it's done more for me than I could have ever imagined. I like myself again, and I want to share that with you and with Zach and Damon. I want to live my life like I am here in this moment – alive and open and happy to be living."

"You weren't happy to be living? You weren't happy?" John asks me with fear and hurt.

"I wasn't living. I was just getting through my days. I'm going to be better now. I'm going to sew more and see what I can do to be creative and develop something for me that makes me happy. You're going to see more of the Gail you married again, I promise."

I walk over to him and put my arms around him. We wrap into each other with a hunger that is familiar and yet has been absent for too long. I pull my head back to reach up and kiss him. There are no other lips like John's lips. His kiss was made for me. Our mouths and body make connections that remind me of the rewards to be had with living an awake life. My hands explore his back and shoulders. I love his body. I remember one of my favorite aspects of his body and reach down to grab his backside. This brings his arms around me tighter and his pelvis into me. He's working to put as much of himself as he can in contact with me. I think for a second that we may drop to the floor when I hear a person behind me clear her throat.

"UHM-uhm, sorry, um, you know there are sleeper berths on this vessel," says Sheriff Tracy.

I give this information serious consideration. I look up at John and see that he's ready to run for an open berth as well. I turn to ask Sheriff Tracy where we can find the rooms, when I see Steve coming up the stairs. I feel John's hand grip my arm and know that he sees Steve too.

John stoops a bit so his mouth is closer to my ear to say, "Seriously, did the guy you leave with have to be that good-looking?"

I give John's middle a good poke with my elbow, which causes him to utter an *oof* and straighten up.

"Steve, come here and meet John," I say. Steve walks over to us and puts his hand out to shake John's. Their hands connect but neither of them speaks. Their silence and firm grip on each other's hands starts to weird me out after a few seconds. "Aren't either of you going to say anything?"

"I'm waiting to see if he yells at me," Steve replies, "which is fine, by the way." He turns to John. "If you need to yell at me, please go ahead."

"I'd like to yell at you," says John. "I've been rehearsing yelling at you for most of today. No, honestly, I rehearsed hitting you." I can see Steve's grip get a little tighter around John's hand, probably trying to keep John from forming a fist. "Don't worry. I'm not going to hit you," John continues. "I don't think I'm going to yell at you either... yet." John lets go of Steve's hand. Steve takes half a step back, just in case.

"Thank you for not hitting me, or yelling at me yet," says Steve. "I just want to say to you, so we're clear, that Gail rescued me. I may have come up with the idea that took her out of San Francisco for a day, which I think turned out well for her." Steve turns to me for affirmation, and I nod my head in agreement. "But helping her out of the city helped me out of a depression I've been carrying. I understand why I'm not your favorite person, but today was necessary, and I don't regret it. I am sorry that it hurt you."

John takes a few seconds with Steve's explanation and apology before he says to Steve, "I may like you someday. I just can't like you right now."

Steve nods his head that he understands and takes a few steps away from us.

I reach out and take John's hand. As my fingers mesh with his and we look into each other's eyes, fireworks go off around us. John's eyes are filled with love for me. He sees the same boundless love for him reflected in my eyes. This connection between us is orders of magnitude more rewarding at the end of my adventure than the Celebration of Light fireworks show I spent the whole day traveling to see could possibly be.

Edgar, Edward, Sheriff Tracy, and Steve each filter past us with smiles and hugs, then stand near windows to watch the fireworks. I catch sight of Nellie leaving the cabin. She looks back at me and winks.

"The story will need to wait a while longer," she says. "Ned is in the pilot's cabin, and I want to be there with him." I nod and smile at her.

John and I remain in the middle of the room, absorbed in each other. John's eyes take on an added glint. I know this glint. All of me lights up in response. Together we pass through the cabin, glancing at the others around us watching the fireworks, returning to each other's gaze as we exit the cabin and find a berth.

CHAPTER 27

wo months fly by way too fast. It feels like time screams past me every day. Days are happier, though. My job doesn't feel like it's killing me a little each day anymore, especially since I've negotiated taking off Fridays to whittle down the mountain of vacation time I have accrued. My director thinks it's temporary, like a vacation. I'm working to make it more. I'm using the time to sew and build something new for myself. I'm taking fashion design classes as well. On top of clothes for kids, I've started designing clothes for me and other women like me. My favorite thing to design in all the clothes I make are pockets. It's bothered me for years that pockets seem to be disappearing from women's clothes. We need them. We need lots of pockets, and it's been fun to figure out fashionable ways to display pockets instead of trying to hide them. Though secret pockets are fun too. I designed a secret pocket in a jacket I made and wear almost daily. It holds a napkin from the zeppelin where life started again for me.

John and I built a sewing studio in our guest room. I get up at five a.m. to sew and don't stop until I have to leave for work. John gets the kids ready for school now. It is the time of day when I do what I love. I'm happy and sane as long as I make and take this time for me.

Fridays and the weekends are when I pull all my work together and figure out building my business. The rest of my days goes to kids and husband and work and house and bills and shopping and volunteering and trying to exercise and sometimes, when the planets align, I see my friends. The difference these days is that my heart is in it all.

Today the planets have aligned. Six weeks ago, when an email thread thirty messages long finally ended in a date everyone could make, today's event was set. As the Universe would have it, no one has had to cancel. I get to see all my new friends, my angels, and I have two months' worth of good stuff to share.

As we pull up to the Crepes Fairy eatery, I don't see anyone from our crew sitting outside. They may be inside, or we may be the first. I see the table where Steve and I sat at the start of our grand adventure, and I see that it is open. "I'm going to hop out and grab that table out front," I tell John. "Do you mind?"

"No, go for it, looks great," says John. "I'll park and meet you there with the boys."

I jump out and skip over to the table. I set my jacket on a chair and am about to peek inside to find Edgar when the Crepes Fairy bounces out to greet me. "You're here!" Edgar exclaims as he rushes to me and gives me a big fairy bear hug. "I'm glad you're here first because I've been on pins and needles all day for this." Edgar releases me then takes a step back so I can see all of him. "What do you think of my new accessory, Madam Designer?" In addition to the tights, wings, and suspenders that are classic and standard Crepes Fairy attire, I see that Edgar is wearing a crown.

"It's a beautiful crown!" I proclaim. "You can now ascend to your rightful place as the King of the Crepes Fairies."

"I have always been the King," states the Crepes Fairy, "but now I have a crown to show the rest of the world what I've known to be true inside me all along."

I curtsy to the King to show my respect for his station. "Long may you reign."

"Rise, loyal subject, and sit while I get some menus. John and your boys are coming, right?"

197

"They're here," I tell him. "John is parking the car. They'll walk up any minute."

"Outstanding, back in a tick. I've kept all these front tables open for our party. Nice jacket, by the way." With that, the Crepes Fairy King flits back into his Crepes Kingdom. I sit at my table and enjoy a quiet moment to myself, watching people in my city amble past me. I think back to that day that shifted my perception and brought me back to life. How odd that one day can change my whole outlook, yet life around me seems to go on as it did before. I'd like to ponder on that, but my thoughts are interrupted by a flash of bright pink in my periphery that catches my attention. My head whips around to see Peep walking toward me.

"Gail!" Peep calls out to me. I jump out of my chair and wave.

"I'm so glad you're here," I call back to him. I see Steve, Aria, and Carrie behind Peep. I wave and call out 'hi' to them. Steve and Carrie are holding hands. This is Carrie's third visit to San Francisco in the last six weeks. Steve has also made sure his business client in Vancouver needed to meet with him often and in person. It seems Steve has had a breakthrough idea of using our journey as landscape for a new adventure app. Escaping the burning tunnel is one part of the app I still can't bring myself to watch.

Steve kisses Carrie's hand before releasing her to shuffle past Peep so he can get to me first. He lifts me up into a hug given to family and best friends. We're both now. Though we email often, it's been a month since we laid eyes on each other. Seeing him up close makes it feel like our whole adventure just happened yesterday.

"Did you see my email this morning?" Steve asks me while he still has me a foot off the ground.

"No, I didn't see it before we left. What's up?" Steve puts me down just as Peep and Carrie reach us. Before Steve can answer my question, Peep steps in and gives me a warm hug that I return.

"You look great, Gail," Peep tells me.

"So do you," I say. "Is that a new shade of pink in your hair?"

"No, I just had it done so it looks brighter than when you saw me last," Peep tells me. "I never stray from my signature color. I must be true to the Peep pink."

"That's a great way to be Peep," I tell him. Though most may tire of a strong hair color over time, I get the feeling that Peep will be Peep, pink hair and all, for the whole of his life.

"Back to my email," says Steve.

"Just a sec," I tell him. "I haven't said hi to Carrie and Aria. Hello, ladies," I say to them and give each a quick hug.

"Okay, Steve, your email?" But before Steve can answer...

"Hello!" says the Crepes Fairy King as he emerges from his front door with several menus in hand. "I'm so glad to finally meet you, Peep! I've heard good things about you from everyone else standing here. Hello to you again, Carrie, so good to see you. Aria, you've grown. You know the rule against growing up while you're in my restaurant, so stop that right now. Oh good, here's John with the boys."

John comes up beside me and puts an arm around me. Even with beautiful Carrie here, John feels the need to make sure Steve remembers I'm married. They all shake hands to say hi. John puts his hand out to shake Steve's, and Steve grabs John's hand with a look of guarded hope. Neither of them utters a word, again, as they keep their grip on each other.

"The two of you need to find a better way to say hello," I tell them both.

John takes a breath and says, "We'll get there, I suppose, but today steely silence still works for me."

Steve keeps a firm hold on John's hand as he says, "You're good at the steely silence. There's something very Bruce Lee about you." I can see John contemplating this compliment, not sure how he wants to respond. He decides to go with the truth.

"That kind of flattery works on me. Keep it up." And with that they release hands. A baby step of progress is still progress.

Steve turns to me to say something, but then I remember how eager I am to show off. "Hold that thought," I tell him. "Zach, Damon, come here for a sec and let everyone see the outfits I made you. Zach is wearing cargo pants I sewed with custom zippered pockets for his trading cards, little army men toys, and a small pad of paper and a pencil he can use to draw his stories. Zach's shirt is reversible, purple on one side, black on the other. Damon is wearing a custom jumpsuit so he can travel into space or become a Ghostbuster as needed, but I think you'll agree it's stylish enough for him to wear to this restaurant as well." The boys spin for me so people can see them at every angle. Applause breaks out, causing the boys to ham it up with silly faces and aerial twists.

"How fun are these clothes? Do you guys love them?" Steve asks my boys.

"Yeah, Mom did great," says Zach.

"We each have a secret pocket too in our clothes where we can put treasure," Damon announces to the crowd.

"Of course, the secret pocket is supposed to be secret," I say, "but Damon doesn't keep secrets yet, which is just fine."

"You've done beautiful work, Gail, congratulations," says Steve. "All the kids of San Francisco should look so good."

"Well, maybe one day they will, along with their mothers. I'm wearing my favorite new clothes as well today," I happily boast. Behind Steve, I see the rest of our party approaching. I wave past him to Nellie and Ned, Sheriff Tracy and her husband, Henry, Giuseppe and Juliette, and Edward. The gang is all here. The Crepes Fairy King gets us all seated around tables with menus before he gets our attention to make an announcement. "Everyone, please order whatever grabs your fancy but save some room. You will be the first to sample a new crepe I've been developing, and I want your opinions in particular on this one."

The Crepes Fairy flies back into his restaurant, leaving us to look over the menus. Steve, who is sitting next to me at our table leans over to talk. "About my email this morning…"

"Right, sorry, what was in your email?" I ask him.

"Things are going very well with Carrie," Steve informs me.

"I can see that. Your kids will be outrageously beautiful."

"It's a little soon for that, but thanks. What we are doing is making plans a few months out into the future now instead of just a few days or weeks. We're planning a trip to Alaska as a winter holiday."

"That sounds cold," I respond, "but I'm sure you'll have a great time. Why Alaska?"

"We'd both like to see the Iditarod race. It just seems so crazy. We want to see it for ourselves, and we're taking Aria."

"That's fantastic! Good for you," I say. "I'm jealous, though I don't think I'd be great with the cold."

"Don't be jealous. Plan something for your family. If I know anything about you, Gail, I know you're a good traveler," Steve affirms, and he's right. I am a mighty traveler.

Waiters come to take our orders. I can't decide between the Charlie Chaplin or the Mr. Bean crepe, which are both incredible in their own right. I decide to get my usual, the Strawberry Fields. It seems appropriate for today. It was the crepe that started my grand day off right.

As our waiters leave to get our meals ordered, three more waiters come outside with plates in their hands. They line up to the side of our tables. Our royal Crepes Fairy follows them with a plate in his hands. "Ladies and Gentlemen," booms the Crepes Fairy, "it is with great joy that I present to you the latest and greatest crepe to be created by yours truly. I give you, the Zelda!" A couple of plates are placed on each table so we can share in this latest marvel. The Zelda crepe is shaped like the zeppelin aircraft that carried us through the end of our journey, and is even sprinkled with silver dust to make the resemblance truly remarkable. We all applaud this work of art. "Thank you, thank you, but wait until you try it," trumpets the Crepes Fairy. "Inside the Zelda is a strong, saucy blend of Camembert cheese mixed with a hint of Stilton, shreds of ham, apricots, and crushed pecans. I chose these distinct ingredients for the Zelda because they not only came together to make a beautiful combined taste, but also because they represent the bold, nutty, odd, yet working combination that was our Zelda crew. It is folded, as you can see, into the shape of our air chariot, dusted with silver for effect, and topped with lines of black cherry reduction to give her definition in both her look and her taste. *Bon appétit.*"

We dig into our zeppelins, and all around me I hear yummy sounds emanating from mouths full of gooey, nutty goodness. The Crepes Fairy has done it again. As I take my third bite of Zelda, I think to myself that I should slow down since I have another crepe coming, but decide that I can just get that in a box for home. I turn to John, who is sitting on the other side of me from Steve.

"Want to go on an adventure with me?" I ask him.

"Yes, I want to go on an adventure with you." John is grinning ear to ear. These words make him very happy.

"Let's go somewhere new and do something different," I propose, "and let's leave the kids with my parents."

John drops his fork onto his plate and puts both his hands on either side of my face. He brings my face to his and gives me a long, loving kiss.

"I want to leave tomorrow," John whispers, "but I guess we should plan it out."

"I don't know," I say. "Let's see what happens tomorrow."

We kiss again. This kiss is slower and sweet. Zach and Damon both let out an *ewwwwwww* from across the table, but kids need to see what a life lived and loved looks like. As it turns out, I'm able to show them.

DEDICATION

Thank you
Nicholas John Warwick Donaldson
for your belief in me, your support, your kindness, and for making me
giggle every day.

From your grateful wife
Rebecca Gail Moutray Donaldson

Thank you
Charles E. Polly
for teaching me to write from my heart.

ACKNOWLEDGMENTS

Working with Kristen Tate of the Blue Garret gave me the confidence to publish this book. Her work as Content Editor and Copy Editor is immeasurable.

The book cover art is the beautiful work of Caroline Wiryadinata.

ABOUT THE AUTHOR

RGM Donaldson is a debut novelist living in the San Francisco Bay Area with her husband and two boys.

Visit www.rgmdonaldson.com to learn more about RGM Donaldson. Join the mailing list on the website to stay informed about the author and her work.

www.ingramcontent.com/pod-product-compliance
Lightning Source LLC
Chambersburg PA
CBHW070834120626
46556CB00002B/750